PLAYBOY'S REWARD

TENNESSEE THUNDERBOLTS

GINA AZZI

THREE CITIES PUBLISHING LLC

*For my husband Tony — You're my favorite cover model.
And I'll forever be your friend-girl. Love you.*

Playboy's Reward

Copyright © 2022 by Gina Azzi

ONE

HARPER

THE SOUND of my keys ricocheting off the little dish on the console table clangs loudly in my empty condo. Not just empty, lonely. My bag slips off my shoulder and thuds on the bare floor.

I sigh, flipping on the foyer lights before locking the door behind me.

I'm grumpy. Exhausted. And hangry as hell.

I kick off my heels on the way to the kitchen and peer into the refrigerator, the light illuminating another type of emptiness.

"I forgot to get groceries," I mutter to myself, shutting the refrigerator door.

Sighing again, just because I feel like it, I uncork a bottle of red wine, pour myself a generous glass, and open the Uber Eats app on my phone.

I scroll through the options. Salads and sandwiches, pizzas and burgers, sushi and...my stomach rumbles. I order the jalapeño poppers and nachos, extra beef, extra guac, extra cheese. And a Coke. I deserve a Coke.

Once my order is confirmed, I drop my phone on the

kitchen counter, walk around my condo, flipping on lights and opening the blinds I forgot about this morning in my mad dash to make it out the door on time for work. I enter my bedroom, wriggle out of my pencil skirt and blouse, and toss on some leggings and a baggy T-shirt from college. Pulling my hair up in a high ponytail, I relocate to my living room, grab my wine glass, and sink into my favorite chair, staring out at Downtown Knoxville.

Nearly a year ago, I moved back to Tennessee, only twenty minutes from the town I grew up in, as a result of a job offer I couldn't turn down and my mother's incessant nagging that it's time to come home.

Nearly every weekday since, I've dragged my ass out of bed at the crack of dawn to work out, run, or move my body in some way. In the past eleven months, I've made investments and saved money, donated to animal rescue centers, and started journaling. I have an eleven-year-old pen pal in Thailand. I shop local.

And I've never been lonelier.

I gulp my wine, frustrated that so many nights end like this—me, drinking wine, in my living room, alone. My days at work are fulfilling; I love my job. I love working with the Coyotes franchise. I love football...and men who play football.

But now that I'm working for the team, I've drawn a line in the sand. I'm not hooking up with any of the players. That commitment, along with the hours I'm logging at the office, have made my dating life nonexistent.

But who cares if I haven't dated? I've fantasized about my sexy neighbor who lives on the floor above mine, ahem, the penthouse. Does that count as something? Sometimes, if I crane my neck the right way, I can see him sipping a scotch on his balcony, his easy laughter comforting. More often than not, he's got a hot woman with him but who am I to judge? Instead, I take a cold shower and meditate before bed.

I'm *trying*, dammit.

But I am exhausted of trying so damn hard to fit into my old life as a new woman. I haven't fully let go of the anger, the bitterness, the resentment of my past. Of memories that unfolded in my childhood town, on my parents' front lawn.

I certainly haven't moved on enough from the betrayal to connect with my old, high-school friends. Nor have I put myself out there to forge new friendships with other like-minded, career-oriented women in Knoxville.

Instead, I'm in a rut. I'm pushing myself in all aspects of life except the one that truly matters: community. Right now, I have none and the loneliness of that gnaws at me.

I glare at my bag by the front door, recalling its contents. I blame the envelope inside for my current state.

An invitation to my ten-year high-school reunion.

Ugh. I gulp my wine.

Moving back to Tennessee, even to the city, was agonizing. Would I run into Sean? Does Anna mention me anymore? Does she miss my friendship the way I sometimes miss hers? Does Sean tell the women he dates now that he's a cheater? Do they hear the gossip?

Of course, I could ask Mom for the details of Sean's or Anna's lives. But my childhood crush, turned high-school sweetheart, turned college love cheating on me with my forever best friend, cultivating a relationship with her behind my back the semester I studied abroad, announcing that he was marrying her when I returned home, gutted me from the inside out.

They called their wedding off two months before she

walked down the aisle and even that didn't provide the vindication I wanted. I don't know if anything ever will.

Their betrayal leveled me, and the scars of their manipulation and lies pushed me from Tennessee to Chicago for six years. Until the job offer—Creative Director of Marketing with THE Knoxville Coyotes, the pride and joy of Southern football—coincided with one of Mom's begging sessions and I caved.

I moved back. I threw myself into work and bettering myself and growing stronger. I've made a hell of a lot of progress too. But that invitation is my undoing.

I polish off my wine and pour another glass.

This is just a weak moment. It won't last. I can wallow in wine and guac tonight and snap back tomorrow. I'll run an extra mile in the morning. The lights outside my window blur and fuck, am I crying?

Swiping a hand over my cheek confirms that I am. I tip my head back and stare at the ceiling instead, willing the tears to reabsorb into my eyeballs. I don't want to be weak. I don't want to care this much. I want to move on and embrace the kick-ass life I'm building for myself in a city that I've loved my whole life.

Besides, I could just not go and save myself the stress, the heartache, the hurt of showing up solo. Because everyone in my town bet that Sean and I would end up together. We were the golden couple—football quarterback and dance team captain, prom king and queen. Anna Drew stabbing me in the back was a plot twist no one saw coming but the town ate it up like handfuls of popcorn during an intense drama. Or, in my case, a psychological thriller.

Yeah, I'm not going. See, that was easy. Decision made.

I release the breath I've been holding. I'm being dramatic and I know it but...can't I give into self-pity tonight? While Mom knows how hard the loss hit me, she doesn't know how much hurt I still drown in. My college friends know Sean and Anna's engagement sent me spiraling, but no one realizes how deep I've sunk.

It's been years. I should be over it. I should be thriving. And most days, I'm faking it enough to believe it. But not tonight. No, tonight proved I'm not ready to see them, and so I will decline the invitation. The people I *want* to talk to from high school, I keep in touch with. One of my old acquaintances, Leo, just signed with the Coyotes and is back in town. We had coffee the other day. Why do I have to see anyone else, when I haven't bothered to reach out to them in the past five years?

I don't. I'm done compromising pieces of myself to fit in, to adapt to anyone's version of who I *should* be. I'm just me and that needs to be enough.

The shrill ring of my phone interrupts my thoughts and I force myself to stand from the chair and dig around my purse.

"Of course," I murmur when I see Mom's name on the screen. "Hello?"

"Harper, you didn't call."

"I just got home thirty minutes ago." A knock sounds on the door and I cradle the phone between my shoulder and cheek as I gratefully accept dinner from the Uber Eats delivery guy.

Mom clucks her tongue. "Working this late? If you could just settle down with a good man, you wouldn't have—"

"I love my job," I cut her off. Working for the Coyotes is a dream come true. My passion for football started long before my romance with Sean. It was born out of my Dad's love for the game and even though I lost Sean, I kept football.

"I know," Mom mutters. "What?" she calls out and I smirk, knowing she's fielding one of Dad's questions. "Your father wants to know how many season tickets you get this year."

I laugh. "I already told him, still two. And we have the whole summer to discuss next season."

Mom chuckles with me. "You know how he is."

"Obsessed."

"Proud," she corrects me, and I grin. When I took the job with the Coyotes, it's possible Dad was more excited than me.

"Thanks, Mom. So, what's going on?" I sink down to the floor, set the poppers and nachos on the coffee table, and dig in.

Mom's quiet for a long moment and my stomach sinks because I know what's coming.

I open my mouth, but she beats me to it.

"Your high-school reunion is in two weeks," she feigns casual, but I know that she knows exactly what she's doing.

"I'm not going," I blurt out. Rip off that Band-Aid.

"Harper June—"

"Don't middle name me. I'm an adult. If I decide I don't want to see anyone I graduated with, it's—"

Mom's scoffing halts me. "Anyone? Or two specific people?"

"Mom," I groan. "I'm not ready."

"Harper, you live here now. You're going to run into them eventually. Wouldn't it be better to get it over with? You're all adults now...maybe you can find some closure."

"Closure," I mutter. What the hell is that? "I don't want to go," I say firmly.

"I RSVP'd for you," Mom announces, guilt threading her tone.

My heart rate spikes, and a shudder runs through me. "Mom!"

"Harper, it's time. You have your dream job in your dream city near your family. You can't avoid Sean and Anna—"

I blanche at the sound of their names spoken aloud and together.

"Forever," Mom carries on, ignoring my gagging. "At least at the reunion, you have your other friends to lean on. It won't catch you off guard. And you can move on. Come home more, not just counting Sunday dinners. Truly live here, in Knoxville, and spend time with your family and friends without looking over your shoulder."

"Who did you tell I'm going?"

"Karen Drew."

I squeeze my eyes shut. Of course Anna's mom is part of the organizing committee. She was always a super involved parent—Class Mom, Head of the PTA, Organizer for Football Boosters.

"She asked if you're bringing a date," Mom adds and my eyes pop open.

I hold my breath, fearful of Mom's response. What's worse? Going stag or going with a date I beg to accompany me?

Who would I even ask?

Jeremiah pops into my mind. He'd have to drive up from Atlanta, and take off work, but I know he'd do it. Because he's still hoping that something will develop between us, even though we haven't had sex in over five months. Damn, I can't ask him and give him mixed signals.

A few of the single guys on the Coyotes would do me a

solid, but that would cause so much speculation that...no, I drew the line in the sand! I can't mix my professional life with my in-shambles personal one.

"I said yes," Mom announces, a quiet indignation in her tone.

It makes me smile, knowing that Mom is on my side. She may be trying to tough love me but deep down, she hates what Sean and Anna did.

"So bring someone sexy," she demands.

I choke on my wine.

Mom snorts. "It's time, Harper. You can do this."

I continue my coughing and drain my second glass. "I don't want to."

"I know. But sometimes, we have to do things we don't want to do. It's called growing up."

"It sucks."

Mom laughs. "I love you, Harp. Let me know if you want to go dress shopping together."

I roll my eyes and exchange good nights with my mom. Then, I chug another glass of wine, enjoying the numbness that spreads through my body. Except it gives way to hurt when I dig the invitation out of my bag. My hurt morphs into anger at the way Sean and Anna treated me.

And, fuck, besides Jeremiah who will end up being too complicated of a date, what sexy man can I bring as a plus-one?

My dating pool is so shallow, it's pretty much dried up.

Pouring my fourth glass of wine, I stalk out to my balcony, the humid heat hitting my cheeks.

I grip the railing and stare out at the city lights.

Then, I open my mouth and scream.

"Fucking motherfuckerrrrrrrrr!"

TWO

DAMIEN

AS A COLORFUL PROFANITY cuts the air, I move to the edge of my balcony. A trickle of fear drips down my spine at the heartache in the screamer's tone, erasing the calm I felt moments ago and setting me on edge.

I frown when I spot my sexy-as-sin downstairs neighbor. Haylee, Harlow... Her name is something like that. Quirky but strong.

Harper.

Right now, Harper is heaving deep breaths, her head bent, wine sloshing over the rim of her glass.

I take a swig of my scotch and lean over my railing, studying the petite brunette as her shoulders shake with anger and something else...something that causes my chest to tighten painfully.

My brother, Charlie, has experienced moments of reckless desperation, more since his engagement ended, and it always hurts to see someone struggle with their pain.

She shudders out another breath. "Fuck, fuck, fuck," drops from her mouth like a chant. Or a plea.

I clear my throat.

Her body locks down and slowly, she peers up at me. Her eyes—a brilliant blue, like the hottest part of a flame—blaze before she snaps them closed. Her cheeks redden. "How much of that did you hear?"

I blow out a breath, my worry easing at the sass in her tone. "The motherfucker or the fuck, fuck, fuck part?"

She swears again.

My smirk widens into a smile. "You okay?"

Her eyes open. "What do you think?"

I stare at her. Her eyes are fierce, her hair is pulled up on top of her head, one of those high ponytails that reminds me of cheerleaders in high school. She's rocking a baggy-ass T-shirt and sheer leggings and still, she's a ten. A fifteen.

I shake my scotch, the lone ice cube clinking against the glass.

My hockey team, the Thunderbolts, didn't qualify for the Second Round of play-offs. Tomorrow, I have no practice. No mandatory weightlifting. Nothing to do but hang out and enjoy a couple months of summer.

While I usually avoid female drama, Harper, a woman I've eye-fucked from afar for the better part of the past year, seems to be more enticing than theatrical. Definitely someone I can pass time with and enjoy her presence. Get lost in it, maybe in her.

"I think you should come up for a drink."

Her eyes widen, her lips parting. Her nose ring, a cerulean stud, glints in the moonlight.

I chuckle. I like that I've surprised her.

She bites her bottom lip, and my chuckle dies because fuck me, she's sexy.

"I'm about to finish off a bottle of wine," she admits slowly.

"Bring the bottle with you." I lift an eyebrow. Will she agree or blow me off?

She tilts her head, as if studying me. "Give me five minutes."

"See you in five," I agree. "Code's 2413." I toss out the elevator code since I live in the penthouse.

I wait for her to move back into her apartment before I tear into mine, cleaning it up as best as I can. I toss dirty dishes in the dishwasher. I stuff dirty clothes in the hamper. I tidy the stupid throw pillows my teammate's girlfriend, Maisy Stratford, purchased to warm up my living space. I may have groaned when she showed up with them, but she was right. Girls appreciate the homey touch.

The elevator dings, the doors opening.

I turn to see Harper clutching a bottle of red wine and balancing two takeout containers on one hand.

"You didn't have to bring food," I say, moving toward her and reaching out to take the containers.

"I'm still eating dinner." She places the wine bottle on my kitchen counter and surveys my space. "Nice digs."

"Thanks," I snort, liking how cool she plays it. Or maybe she's not impressed at all, which makes me like her even more.

As an NHL player hailing from old Connecticut money, living in a penthouse, most women like tangling up because of the novelty of my profession or the obvious display of my financial security. But this woman seems more lost in her own thoughts than anything related to me.

"I'm Harper." She holds out a hand. "Harper Henderson."

"I like the alliteration." I shake her hand. She rolls her eyes. I grin. "Damien Barnes."

"Nice to meet you. Officially."

"Yeah." I move around the kitchen counter to pour her a glass of wine and refill my scotch. "You moved in a year ago, right?"

"A year next month." She slides onto a barstool and opens the takeout containers. "We've got poppers and nachos."

I place a wine glass in front of her. "This is dinner?"

"For tonight, yeah."

"Rough day?"

She shrugs one shoulder and bites into a nacho. "You could say that."

It's clear she doesn't want to talk about it and with any other woman, I'd back off. But something about Harper Henderson entices me. "Work stuff?"

She pins me with a look that borders on a glare. "Personal shit."

"Of the romantic variety?" I press, swiping a jalapeño popper because the season is over and I can indulge in all the shit I usually stay away from.

Harper sighs. "My ten-year high-school reunion is in two weeks."

"Oh." I chew the popper and nearly choke as the heat of the jalapeño hits me.

Harper rolls her eyes again and slips from her barstool, moving around me and navigating my kitchen like she's been here before—shit, has she? Nah, I'd remember if she crashed one of my parties. She passes me a glass of water.

"Thanks," I mutter as I gulp it. "You hated high school?" I guess, once my coughing is under control. She doesn't look like the type to have hated it. She looks like one of the girls who ruled the hallways but...maybe I'm reading her wrong?

"No, I loved it," she admits, a thread of nostalgia in her tone.

I lift my eyebrows.

Amusement flickers in her eyes. "You don't quit, do you?"

"Never." I smile.

She shakes her head, but a little grin plays over her lips. "My high-school boyfriend, the one I dated for most of college and thought I'd marry, hell, everyone in our town had been planning our wedding since we were like twelve—"

"That guy." I nod, knowing exactly who she's talking about. The one who is the standout, golden kid that all the girls want to fuck and all the guys want to emulate. My brother, Charlie, comes to mind. At least, the version of him before his relationship went to hell and he started partying too hard. He can still turn it around but if he keeps going at the pace he is, he'll end up losing a hell of a lot more than his ex-fiancée and position at Dad's company.

"He cheated on me with my childhood best friend the semester I went abroad—"

"Damnnnnn."

"And then proposed to her."

"Shit." I peer at her, hating the ripples of hurt that bleed over her expression.

Harper sighs. "They called off the wedding. It's been years and still...I don't want to see them. Nor do I want to face everyone else from my graduating class as they stare at me, waiting to see how I react. Do I greet Anna with a hug? Do I ignore Sean? Do I inquire about their personal lives?"

"Just...don't go," I offer.

She snaps her fingers, pointing at me as she sips her wine. Her elbow falls off the countertop and I bite back my chuckle. Harper Henderson is tipsy and it's pretty adorable. "Exactly. I was going to decline but my mom—"

I groan knowing what's coming.

"She RSVP'd for me."

"Your mom should meet mine," I commiserate, sipping my scotch.

Harper snorts. "Yeah, well she's RSVP'd to Anna's *mom*, and included an imaginary plus-one I now need to pull out of my ass like freaking Houdini." She drains her wine glass.

I tip my head to check out her ass. "Your ass is much nicer."

She laughs, her eyes flashing. I straighten, the sound of her laughter hitting me hard. It's a strong laugh with a thread of breathlessness, and already I want to hear it again. I clear my throat. "That shit's harsh," I agree, feeling bad for Harper because she seems so stressed, genuinely worried about rocking up to this reunion at all, never mind solo.

She moves to refill her glass but the bottle's drained, so I uncork another one, passing her a full glass. "The reunion is here, in Knoxville?"

"Thanks." She accepts the wine. "Yeah, I grew up about twenty minutes from here. They were supposed to hold it downtown at the Premier Hotel—"

"Fancy."

She smirks. "But there are so many people coming in from out of town that want to see our school again so...it's just at my old high school. Like homecoming and prom." A wistful look crosses her face. "A throwback kinda night."

I drop my elbows to the top of the island, moving into her personal space.

Harper looks up, her eyes holding mine prisoner, but

she doesn't back away. She waits me out, and God, I like it. Her fire, her challenge, *her*.

"You should take me."

Her eyes flare in disbelief before she laughs. "What?"

"I'll be your plus-one." I pluck a nacho and stuff it in my mouth before I move even closer, drawn to her plush lips, the scent of her skin. Coconut and sunshine.

She narrows her eyes at me, shifting closer, our faces inches apart. "Seriously?" Her tone is breathy, laced with disbelief and a halting kind of hope that makes my heart hurt for her.

This is the last woman that should be publicly humiliated for falling for the wrong guy. One who clearly doesn't deserve her.

"Seriously," I say, committing to the event. What do I have to lose? It's the kind of thing I've done for friends or teammates' little sisters and cousins in the past. I'm an exceptional plus-one and have proved it at countless weddings, a few charity galas, and once, a funeral.

Harper's hands dart out and she grips my T-shirt. She tugs me over the countertop and I stumble forward, caught off guard. Surprise rips through me as her mouth lands on mine.

I grab her upper arms to keep from falling forward on the counter. A warning rolls through my mind—she's vulnerable, tipsy, overwhelmed—but then her tongue runs along the seam of my lips, and I part them, falling into the kiss faster than I volunteered to be her date.

She kisses me hard and I shift, my hand cupping her cheek as I angle her head. I move around the counter, and she turns into me, her thighs parting for me to step between them. She doesn't break our connection and neither do I. Instead, I savor her lips, this kiss.

Harper pulls me under. She's equal parts soft and hard, sweet and fierce. She's intoxicating and confusing. Captivating and complicated.

She pulls back and I release her, my hand slipping down her arm until I can hold on to her wrist.

"You can still back out," she offers.

And I laugh. The sound surprises both of us because it's so sincere. "I'm not going to back out, Harper."

"But"—her brow furrows—"what's in it for you?" Her cheeks blaze the moment the words are out of her mouth as her gaze darts down.

Immediately, I feel like a piece of shit. I drop her wrist and shuffle back a few steps, gripping the back of my neck. "Look, that kiss was hot, but we never have to kiss or touch again. I'm coming because...we're neighbors."

She arches an eyebrow, as if she doesn't believe me.

"And I'm a Good Samaritan," I continue.

She smirks.

"I've been checking you out hard for nearly a year."

Her eyes narrow. "Yet you've never done anything about it."

I laugh again. Damn, this woman is surprising. Refreshing. "That's because of my job. And...your proximity," I admit. My focus is on hockey all the time. I only indulge in hook-ups, and sleeping with a woman who lives on the floor beneath mine is a type of drama I've learned to steer clear from. "Look, I've got nothing going on for the next two months. Most of my teammates headed back to their hometowns for the summer and—"

"Your teammates?"

Seriously? I bite my tongue before I voice that. "I play hockey."

She stares at me blankly.

I laugh again. Who is this girl? "For the Thunderbolts."

Understanding dawns and she chuckles, shaking her head. "Really?"

"Left wing."

"Wow, I, um, had no idea." She tilts her head, her eyes latched to mine. "Are you sure you want to show up to a high-school reunion with me? People will talk."

I shrug. "I don't put much stock in what people think."

"I wish I was more like you," she says, a thread of hurt in her tone.

"I think you're pretty great the way you are."

"You don't really know me."

"No," I agree. "But I've got two weeks to learn as much as I can."

"If we do this, go to the reunion together, I don't want you to feel uncomfortable or obligated to—"

"I'll be the best fake boyfriend you've ever had," I promise, going above and beyond to prove—what? That she deserves better? More than what she had in the past? I close the space between us and drop my hand to her knee. "Listen, I don't do relationships. There are no big complications in my life. I don't have a girlfriend. The guys on my team, and their girls, will tell you that I'm fun to hang with. I'm not going to overthink this one way or the other. You need a date, and I can be that for you. I can already tell we'll have a good time. It will be fun night and"—I pause, shrugging—"at the very least, we're neighbors who could be friends." I point out to the balcony. "I see you, drinking on your balcony, every time I'm drinking on mine."

"We could be drinking buddies," she surmises, a hint of a smile on her face.

"We could be something, Harper."

"Starting as a fake couple." She bites her bottom lip again.

I hold up my scotch. "We'll be relationship goals."

She laughs and clinks her glass against mine. "Okay, let's do it. Thank you, Damien."

I smile, liking how my name sounds in her voice. Liking how she looks at me with admiration instead of reverence.

"To high-school reunions," I say, tipping back my glass.

Harper laughs again and it's like music, sweeter than anything I've heard in a long time.

THREE

HARPER

A LOW WHISTLE cuts the air as I settle the squat bar back on the rack.

Turning to glance over my shoulder, I smirk at Damien. "Like what you see?"

The corners of his mouth turn upward. "More than you know, Henderson."

I laugh, toss my towel over my shoulder, and move toward him. "I've never seen you work out here before."

"Yeah," he agrees, sitting down on a bench. "I usually work out at the arena—"

"Right."

"But since it's about forty minutes away and I'm on summer holiday..." He takes a swig of his water.

"This is more convenient," I finish his sentence.

"And has better views." His eyes zero in on my ass and I laugh again.

If it was any other guy, I'd blow him off. I hate cheesy lines and obnoxious flirting. But with Damien, it's more playful than serious. It's as if he's trying to get me to laugh more than make me feel uncomfortable.

It's...easy. Even me throwing myself at him, a little bit drunk and a lot desperate, and looking like a fool—first weeping, then kissing him—hasn't diminished how comfortable I feel in his presence.

It's been a handful of days since Damien agreed to be my plus-one and, instead of backing out or trying to put space between us, he's gone out of his way to see me more.

I sit down across from him and stretch out.

"You almost done?" He selects the dumbbells he needs and settles into a set of Arnold presses.

"Yeah." I roll out my neck. "Hitting the showers."

Damien snorts, his eyes flashing to mine.

"That wasn't an invitation," I toss out, partly wishing it was.

Gah! What is wrong with me? Clearly, I'm having sex withdrawals. I could have taken Jeremiah up on his last offer but—no, not going there.

My nice, considerate neighbor has agreed to do me a solid and instead of being thankful for that, I'm ogling him. But, damn, Damien Barnes is hot.

Of course, I Googled him after I clued into who he is and...the internet does not do the man justice. On the ice, he's fire.

But up close and personal...Damien is an inferno.

He grunts as he shifts exercises and I try not to drool.

Damien has dark hair, a brownish-black, that is clipped short on the sides and back but left longer on top. Usually, he works product through it but right now, at the gym, it's natural. Soft. The kind of hair I could run my fingers through.

He drops the dumbbells and moves over to the squat rack. I should move. I should *go*. I do nothing of the sort.

"You sure?" He looks over, his bicep popping as he maneuvers the weight.

"About what?" I force my eyes up to his.

He smirks, his green eyes bright with amusement. "The invitation?"

I groan, smacking myself in the forehead. How obvious am I?

Damien chuckles, the sound easy, as he begins to squat.

"Jesus," I mutter, my eyes glued to his ass.

His shoulders shake with silent laughter since he knows exactly what I'm doing.

I sit down on the bench he vacated and stare, too impressed to be properly embarrassed because— "You should never work out here again."

Another snicker as he racks the bar. Tossing an arm over the top, he leans forward. "Too distracting?" He runs a palm over the stubble coating his jawline and the raspy sound rings in my ears like a motorcycle.

Damien Barnes is more than distracting. He's downright captivating and he knows it.

"Too everything," I admit, moving my hand in a circle to encompass his entire being. I stare straight at him, the teasing gone from my tone.

Damien holds my gaze, his eyes boring into mine with a seriousness he doesn't usually show. "Have lunch with me today."

"I—okay," I agree, trying to keep up with the conversation shift.

"I'll be done in an hour. I'll knock on your door."

I scurry to stand. "I'll be ready."

He smiles. "You already look beautiful, Henderson. Don't overdo it or I'll have to compete with all the other men checking you out."

I scoff. As if there's any competition when he's around?

I grab my water bottle and move toward the exit. "One hour?" I confirm, glancing over my shoulder.

Damien is blatantly checking out my ass and I blush. His eyes roll to mine slowly, not embarrassed for being caught. "One hour."

I exit the gym, taking my time to enter the elevator and press the button for my floor. But once the door to my apartment is locked behind me, I spring into action.

One hour! I sprint into the bathroom and waste an absurd amount of time trying to peel my sweaty sports bra off before flinging myself in the shower. While the hot water beats down on my body, I mentally flip through my closet for clothing options that balance fun with friendship.

I may enjoy Damien Barnes's light teasing and flirty personality. I may have kissed him in a moment of recklessness. But I *can't* cross any serious lines.

I *can't* fall for him.

Because he told me up front that he doesn't do serious. Or girlfriends. Or commitment.

He's a Good Samaritan helping out a neighbor in need.

And I'm a girl who doesn't let my guard down often but when I do...I go all in. I've always been an all-or-nothing kind of woman. With relationships, which is why my experience is capped at three boyfriends—two in middle school followed by Sean. With friendships, which is why I don't have many close bonds in Tennessee. With exercise; I run every morning or not at all for weeks on end. Even with school; I was completing extra credit assignments or barely getting by. Moderation is tough for me, and Damien is way too tempting. If I invest in him, in having a relationship with him, I'll be devastated when he eventually ends it. I'll be even emptier than I am now.

Can't. Go. There.

Can't compromise for anything less than all. The next relationship I commit to will be serious, meaningful, *real*.

When Damien turns his flashing eyes and sexy smirk my way, I need to remember that this is nothing more than a budding friendship with a side of fun.

My heart rate accelerates as I blow-dry my hair. My stomach knots as I slip into a simple sundress that ruffles around my knees and ties on the tops of my shoulders. My breathing ticks up as I slide my feet into sandals and spritz perfume on my inner wrists.

This is lunch, not a date.

He's my neighbor, not my boyfriend.

But then Damien Barnes knocks on my door, and I pull it open.

Surprise widens his eyes as he drinks me in like water during a drought. "Damn, Henderson. You look sexy as hell."

I blush. I swoon. I may even fall a little.

And all my desperate reminders die a thousand deaths.

Because I want Damien Barnes in ways I've never wanted a man before. A part of my lonely, desperate heart wants him for keeps.

———

"HOW LONG HAVE WE BEEN DATING?" he asks over a pitcher of margaritas and an assortment of tacos.

We're at one of my favorite Mexican restaurants and I'm trying—and failing—to play it cool. If I scare Damien off now, I'll lose my date and fail to save face. I just need to get through the next two weeks, the reunion, and then, I can add some distance between myself and my too-hot-for-his-own-good neighbor.

I clear my throat. "I think it's best we stick to facts as much as possible."

"So...two weeks?" He lifts his eyebrows.

I sigh; he's right. We definitely need to embellish. "Seven months."

"Then why weren't you at any of my games?" He points at me with an accusing finger.

I snort. "We were keeping it quiet. Low-key."

"Five months," he decides. "No one knows where the hell they stand the first few months in a relationship but then, once labels are slapped on, they like to backtrack and pretend it was for real from the start."

I pause, thinking that over. "You're right."

"I know," he agrees confidently, popping a chip in his mouth. "This place is incredible."

"Hidden gem."

"I need to hang with you more, Henderson."

"Facts," I agree, trying to appear half as confident as Damien. But his words, the way I want to believe them, sends a shiver of anticipation through my body.

"So, five months?"

I nod. "Five months."

"We met the way we did in real life."

"Yeah, except I wasn't swearing at the night."

Damien chuckles. "Nah. I was spying on you."

I lift an eyebrow, encouraging him to continue.

"Checked you out for weeks, trying to get you to look up at me. But you always played it so cool." He huffs, rolling his eyes in mock annoyance. "So, after weeks of waiting, I finally worked up the courage to—"

"No," I cut him off. "No one will believe that you were too scared to approach *me*."

He looks up from his taco, salsa dripping onto his fingers. "Why not?"

"Why not?" I sputter. Shaking my head, I gesture toward him. "Look at you...and then look at me."

His eyes darken. "Staring straight at you, babe. Trust me, I'd need to work up the courage to chat you up."

I laugh, partly in disbelief, partly in nerves. "No way."

"Fine." Damien sits back in his chair. "At a bar? Nah, I'd approach you because...it's a bar and whatever. But if I really wanted a shot with you, a woman like you—"

"A woman like me?"

"Smart, confident, sexy, independent..." He rattles the adjectives off so quickly, my head spins. "I'd need a game plan."

"So...you spied?"

"Hell yeah." He grins. "And one night, when you walked out onto your balcony, I—"

"Whistled?"

He wrinkles his nose. "I'm a flirt but I wouldn't veer into cat-calling."

I dip my head in agreement.

"I made up some stupid issue with my apartment to see if you had the same issue," he carries on, fabricating this story with such confidence that I half believe him. He snaps his fingers. "A water issue."

"Water?"

"Yeah. So, we get to talking, small talk kind of shit, and I invite you up for a drink."

"And I come up and...realize you made the whole water thing up when I use your bathroom and wash my hands..."

"And you call me on it because you're totally the kind of woman that calls a man on his shit."

I laugh. "That's believable."

"And I shrug and admit I've been trying to talk to you for weeks." His tone is earnest, his expression sweet.

"And I love that you're honest about it so we..."

"Have a drink," he states. "These high schoolers don't need to know you put out on the first date."

My mouth drops open. "Firstly, they're adults."

"Are they?" He arches an eyebrow and I hear the insinuation. If everyone was grown up and acting like adults, my going to the reunion wouldn't be terrifying.

"Secondly, I didn't put out—"

"That kiss was fire."

I blush. "It wasn't a date."

"In this fictional world we're building, it was the first of many."

I blow out a shaky breath, more affected by Damien than I want to be. "Okay, so, we had a drink."

"Mojitos," he confirms. I give him a look and he leans closer. "Someone will ask."

"Have you done this before?" I gesture between us, insinuating our fake relationship.

"Only for the sisters and cousins of my friends." He leans back. "Never for a woman I'm actually attracted to."

My blush deepens.

"And I just grew up in a petty-as-fuck town. I've spent more of the last decade being tossed into galas and events where everyone looks like a million dollars but isn't worth a penny."

"Harsh."

"Call it like I see it, babe."

I squirm in my chair. Damien calling me "babe"

shouldn't affect me. Nothing about this fake date, this regular *lunch*, should affect me. "Then what?"

"Then…we started dating. We kept it casual at first but once the team didn't qualify for the Second Round, we naturally started spending more time together and…"

"Here we are, at a ten-year high-school reunion."

"May I add that we're the best dressed?" He tips his head, picking up his margarita.

"You may." I clink my glass against his. "Because I was voted best dressed in high school."

Damien laughs and takes a long pull. "I was voted biggest flirt."

I grin. "I can totally see it."

FOUR

DAMIEN

"YO." I pick up the phone. "How's relationship bliss?"

"Fuck off," the snarky reply comes, causing me to grin.

"Hi, Damien!" Mila Lewis, my teammate Devon's girl, hollers out.

"Tell Mila I said hey," I reply.

Devon grunts. My grin grows. Devon Hardt is an arrogant, cranky son of a bitch, but under that tough exterior, he's solid. Turned out to be a good captain too, as evidenced by his phone call.

"What can I do for you?" I ask.

He sighs. "Just wanted to say what's up. See how summer's been..."

I chuckle. I'm sure wellness checks make him want to punch something. Still, I answer honestly. "Summer's been all right. Quiet."

"Good quiet or..."

"I'm grabbing a bite with Turner this week." I reference our team goalie, Beau Turner. We're not exactly tight because Turner's a quiet guy with a big family. He mostly keeps to himself or visits his gran and sister. But since we're two of the only guys in downtown for the summer, it will be nice to hang with a teammate.

"Good. Good. Anything else?"

"Been spending time with my neighbor."

Devon mumbles a curse before laughing. "Of course you have. Flavor of the summer?"

I frown, not liking the thought of Harper as something so...fleeting. Even though that's what we are: temporary. "Just friends," I bite out.

Could we ever be more than friends? More than this casual, blurred line thing we've got going on?

The thought of a relationship makes my throat close. I tried that once and it crashed and burned when Brittney realized the depth of my family's dysfunction. We were only in high school, but Brittney had the good sense to cut ties when the ugliness that surrounds the Barnes's social circles started seeping into our relationship.

I've seen the same happen to Charlie and my sister, Fiona. The thought of anything serious after witnessing how my siblings' relationships have altered their lives is downright frightening.

Devon cackles through the line. "Just friends? Bullshit."

I blow out a sigh. "We're...neighbors. Friendly."

"You borrowing some sugar?"

I snort. "I'm escorting her to her ten-year reunion this weekend."

Crickets. Silence. My heart thuds.

"Hardt?" I mumble, wondering if we got disconnected.

Raucous, uninhibited laughter rings in my eardrum. "Shit." I pull the phone away from my ear and stare at it, watching the seconds tick by as Devon practically coughs up a lung.

"Dev, you okay?" Mila's voice rings out again.

"Holy shit," Devon swears. "Baby, get this…"

I roll my eyes.

"Damien is escorting some girl—"

"My neighbor!" I yell.

"To her ten-year reunion," Devon wheezes out in between bursts of laughter.

"Damien?" Mila comes on the line.

"Hey, Mil, how's life?" I ask.

"Not nearly as exciting as yours," she volleys back. "Who is the smart and sophisticated woman that's caught your eye?"

I smirk. "How do you know she's smart and/or sophisticated?"

"Please," Mila mutters dismissively. "No way you're going that far out of your way for a flavor of the week."

I suppress a groan. I guess my causal hook-ups have made the rounds through the team. While it's true, I do mess around, casually date, hook up, whatever, with a lot of beautiful, intelligent, fun women, I never lie to them. I tell them right from the start—this is casual, this is fun, this isn't going anywhere.

But with Harper…it's not going somewhere but it's also not going nowhere.

"Her name is Harper Henderson and—"

"Oh my God! Harper Henderson? She used to be captain of the dance team for West Essex."

"Uh, what?" I mumble, frowning.

Mila laughs. "She's gorgeous! And she can *move*. I mean, she's one hell of a dancer."

"You know her?" Devon says in the background.

"Shh," Mila mutters. "Damien, Harper went to high school a few towns over from mine."

I close my eyes and cluck a sound of agreement. I completely forgot Mila grew up outside of Knoxville.

"Is it your ten-year reunion?" I ask.

Mila laughs. "No, Harper was two years behind me."

"But you know her?"

"Yep," Mila says, her smile evident in her tone. "She dated Sean Collins."

"You sound way too dreamy when you say that cocksucker's name," Devon cuts in.

"He was dreamy...and a fucking douche. Cheated on her in college and ended up engaged to her best friend. People said it was because he knocked her up but...sorry," Mila says suddenly, realizing she's gossiping about Harper.

"Nah, it's cool. She told me the story. That's why she doesn't want to go," I admit.

"Damien Barnes," Mila says my name with an undercurrent of something I can't place.

"Yeah?"

"You're really doing her a solid, you know that?" Sincerity laces Mila's words.

Devon swears again.

"She doesn't deserve this shit; she's a good person," I say, meaning it.

"You're a good person," Mila says softly.

"And I'm the great man who gives it to you," Devon announces before a thud rings out and he swears in pain. "Fucking shit."

"You got him in the nuts?" I ask.

"Oh yeah," Mila responds.

I wince but laugh along with her because sometimes... Devon deserves to be punched in the junk.

"I haven't seen Harper Henderson in years but..." Mila trails off and I can tell she's choosing her words carefully.

"But?" I prod.

"The Harper I remember was awesome. She's not a flavor of the week, Damien."

"No," I agree, a little regretfully. "She's not."

But can she be more than a summer fling? More than a flirty neighbor? More than anything I've ever had before?

I chat for a few more minutes before ending the call.

No, she can't. I've placed Harper firmly in a friends-with-some-benefits box and I need to keep her there. Firstly, because in the past ten days I've really come to enjoy my time with her. If I fuck shit up between us, I'd lose her friendship. And secondly, because I won't *not* fuck shit up with us.

I'd rather have Harper in my life as a tempting, confusing, exciting distraction than nothing at all.

Even if I don't deserve it; even if I'll never deserve her.

———

"YOU'RE STUNNING," I tell her truthfully when she opens the door to her apartment. "And you definitely earned your high-school superlative."

She laughs, shaking her hips. "I went shopping with my mom."

"Your mom has impeccable taste."

"You don't think it's too much?" She holds out her foot, delicately tied with a big, silk bow, and resting on a thin heel that has to be close to four inches. Fuck me.

"Nope," I say, my voice higher than it was a second ago. Images of those shoes wrapped around my lower back, resting on the tops of my shoulders, tossed on my bedroom floor flicker through my mind. "You could never be too much, Henderson."

She gives me a soft smile that makes my chest feel funny, like I might choke. "Let me grab my purse." She moves deeper into her apartment as I loiter by the door, both desperate to check out her shit and holding myself back.

In the past two weeks, Harper and I have spent time together. We've talked about our jobs and our hobbies, exchanged snippets about our families and friends. We've worked out together, had drinks on my balcony, and did random shit around town—grabbed a coffee, checked out a local artisan shop, saw a movie—but I've never spent much time in her space.

Right now, I want to inspect every photo frame as much as I want to bolt out the door. I like spending time with Harper. I like this, her, too much for what it is.

"Damien," she says, looking at me from down the hallway.

"Yeah?" I glance up, get lost in her blue eyes.

"You clean up nicely."

I snort.

She walks toward me, stopping a few feet away. Reaching out, she wraps her slender fingers around my wrist and squeezes. "Thank you for doing this. You have no idea how much this means to me."

My throat tightens, my hands tingle. I nod, too affected by her sincerity to quip.

Harper smiles a brilliant, beautiful smile. "I'm ready when you are."

"Let's do it," I say, placing my fingers in the small of her back. And fuck me, her dress, a deep green that looks modest from the front, is completely open in the back. There's only a small tie around her neck. That's it. With one simple tug, the entire garment would fall to her feet. My hand not touching her curls into a fist.

My fingers itch and I press against her skin. Heat travels up my arm and I pull my fingers away.

Harper seems unaffected by my near meltdown. Thank God.

We step into the hallway and Harper locks up while I avert my gaze and try to get a hold of myself.

What the hell am I doing? I don't act like this. I don't behave so damn...recklessly. Not with my dates. Not with my time. Not with my...heart.

I shake my head to clear my thoughts and lead the way to the parking garage. When Harper sees my ride—a silver Maserati Mom and Dad gifted me for my thirtieth—she sucks in a sharp inhale.

I unlock the door. "This is me, Henderson."

"You don't play, Barnes." She moves to slide into the passenger seat.

Since the seat is low, I take her arm to help her. Her eyes flash to mine—burning blue—and hold. Unable to stop myself, I tug the seat belt across her body and buckle her in.

"No," I agree, my voice rough. "I don't play."

Harper lets out a shaky breath as I close the door and round the car to the driver's side.

Tonight was supposed to be fun and hokey. A silly night to help her save face in front of a bunch of people that judge her for shit that happened years ago.

It doesn't feel fun and hokey anymore.

Instead, it feels meaningful and heavy. It's a hell of a lot more than I bargained for and yet, I want it. I want this with her.

I sit in the driver's seat and start the car. Harper's

breathing is shallow, her fingertips tapping on the center console.

"Hey." I place my hand over hers, curling our fingers into a ball.

She looks at me, panic evident in her eyes.

"We got this, Harper. I promise, you will have fun tonight. I won't let you down."

She works a swallow and nods. "I know."

I give her a lazy grin. "You do?"

She nods again. "I trust you, Damien."

"Good." I squeeze her hand once before releasing my hold and pulling out of the underground garage.

Her words—the sentiment behind them—snaps something into place.

She *trusts* me.

No one ever trusts me. Not truly. I'm the charming, affable, likable guy. Sure, friends confide future plans in me. I'm easy to talk to and rarely judge. But no one trusts me to make their day, a part of their life, better.

Harper Henderson *trusts* me. I won't let her down.

Even if that means protecting her from myself. From my family's bullshit. From my inability to commit and give women what they truly want.

I want to be worthy of her trust. To do that, Harper Henderson needs to be friend-zoned.

FIVE

HARPER

MY PALMS TINGLE WITH NERVES, a clamminess spreading over my skin like a bad hangover, as Damien and I exit his sports car. A sour taste coats my tongue and my heart hammers, loud and erratic, in my chest.

What was I thinking? I can't walk in there.

I can't just stroll into the gymnasium of my high school and pretend like the past six years haven't happened.

The friends who stopped reaching out when Sean chose Anna over me.

The narrowed eyes and wagging tongues of small-minded cliques desperate for gossip.

The memories that taste a hell of a lot more bitter than sweet.

I stall, my steps slowing. My high school looms before me looking physically smaller than I remember and still, I don't want to walk through the double doors. I don't want to see the rows of blue lockers or hear the peals of laughter. I don't want to reminisce and *remember*.

Shit. I can't do this.

I come to a complete halt, my skin breaking out in goose bumps, my mind whirling.

A warm, heavy, steady hand finds the small of my back. Damien brushes the ends of his index and middle fingers up my spine in slow, patient circles.

"You got this, Henderson," he murmurs quietly, his mouth hovering an inch from my ear.

To anyone looking at us, we'd look like lovers caught up in a moment. Damien's body language is casual, but his proximity is both protective and soothing.

I draw in a deep breath and exhale slowly.

"You're a strong, sexy, confident woman. Don't let a guy from high school, or a former friend, determine how much fun you have tonight."

I look up, latch onto his steely green eyes, and let out a slow exhale. How does he know exactly what to say? How is he right?

A soft smirk tugs on the left corner of his mouth. "Besides, you're here with me."

I can't stop myself from smiling. My heart rate slows, feeling returns to my fingers. "What's that mean?"

"You're gonna have a hell of a good time."

I laugh lightly. "Pretty confident, aren't you, Barnes?"

"Gotta be to keep up with you."

I laugh.

He tilts his head, studying me. "Trust me, Harper?"

At the sound of my first name, when he usually quips off my last, I still. I bite my bottom lip, surprised by how easy the word *yes* runs through my mind. I've already told him I trust him and yet, I like that he wants the confirmation.

In two weeks, Damien's restored a lot of the faith I previously lost in members of the opposite sex. "Yes."

"Good. Now let's get in there." He slips his hand from my back and offers it to me. Long, outstretched fingers and a big palm. I slide my hand into his and when he wraps his fingers around mine, a wave of calmness settles over me, eradicating my nerves.

Damien is right. I have just as much a right to be here as Sean or Anna. Just because I left Tennessee doesn't mean this isn't my home. I've been back in Knoxville for a year. Why am I avoiding my hometown? Why am I skipping on visits to my parents' house? I'm not the one who did anything wrong. If anyone should feel ashamed or awkward by my waltzing into that gymnasium, it's Sean and Anna. It's the friends who dropped me faster than a hot potato when Sean's vote on future spouse was cast.

Straightening my spine, I squeeze Damien's hand to let him know I'm okay. I got this. Together, we stride into my high school. The scent—a mixture of paper and glue and cleaning supplies—hits me like a memory. It causes me to smile. I pluck our name cards from a table outside the gym and we enter.

The smile on my face turns genuine when I'm greeted by friendly eyes and a low chuckle.

"Leo! You came." I hug the formidable running back, my old acquaintance turned new friend now that we're both part of the Coyotes franchise.

In high school, Leo rode the bench, hidden behind Sean and his two buddies', Jacob and Oscar, successes on the football field. Leo liked coding and robots, homemade pasta and chocolate milk. He was an anomaly to most of the football team and as such, they ignored him. But now, his presence is too big, his name too meaningful, to be overlooked.

In fact, as my eyes dart around the crowd, I'm relieved

that more eyes are checking out the svelte and sculpted Leo Quincy instead of judging me.

"I didn't think you were going to show," I admit, recalling our conversation over coffee.

Leo shrugs. "My mama made me come."

Laughing, I nod. "Same. I'm glad you're here, Leo."

He dips down and brushes a kiss over my cheek, friendly but also confident, a move he never would have dared in high school. "I'm happy you're back too, Harp." He straightens and holds out a hand to a bewildered Damien. "Leo Quincy."

"The running back," Damien comments, shaking his hand and sizing him up through narrowed eyes. It's no secret that the Tennessee Thunderbolts and the Knoxville Coyotes have a tenuous relationship. But, over the past year, the players have come to regard each other with more warmth and respect, although not yet friendliness. "Damien Barnes."

Leo's eyes light up. "Man, I knew you looked familiar. That was a great goal you had against Chicago in the First Round. I was disappointed y'all didn't advance."

"Oh, thanks," Damien replies, shaking Leo's hand, before returning it to my back.

Leo takes in the movement and shoots me a knowing smirk. I resist rolling my eyes because...is Damien Barnes staking a claim?

Is it because he's my fake date or is there more to his touch?

"Leo Quincy!" Mrs. Riker, the school secretary who I can't believe is still working here, calls out.

Leo grins. "Gotta go. I'll catch up with you, Harp."

"Yeah." I wave as he moves through a throng of faces I mostly recognize.

"Your high-school friend plays for the Coyotes?" Damien asks.

"He's the newest trade. Leo and I were cool in high school, friendly although we traveled in different friend groups."

Damien arches an eyebrow. "I have a hard time believing that Best Dressed and girlfriend of the quarterback didn't mingle with the rest of the football team."

I chuckle and shake my head. "Leo didn't play much in high school. He was very into robotics club and spent his time off the field at the library." I shrug. "Ended up being a walk on in college who—"

"Got one hell of a lucky break when Clemson's running back was injured."

I grin. "So you know a bit of his story. Leo's a nice guy, always has been."

Damien makes a noncommittal sound in his throat, shifting until his entire palm is pressed against the center of my back. I shiver.

I look up just in time to spot Anna making her way toward us, a hesitant smile on her face that would frustrate me if Damien wasn't standing at my side.

She approaches gently, like I'm a ticking time bomb. It annoys me because she deserves my wrath and yet, doesn't she know me well enough to know that I'd never publicly draw more attention to an undesirable situation?

I look down for a moment. No, she doesn't know me any more than I know her, which turned out to be not at all.

Anna's toes, wrapped in sensible black sandals, stop in front of mine.

"Harper, hi," she says quietly, tucking a strand of hair behind her ear the way she does when she's nervous.

I stare at my ex-best friend, trying not to wince at how

familiar she looks. Even without seeing her in six years, she looks the same—a blast from my past I both want to banish and hold on to. She looks pretty, wearing a scarlet wrap dress with delicate, dangly earrings. Her blonde hair is perfectly highlighted, her smile teetering on sincere. It's only her eyes that give away the remorse she feels. Remorse that is genuine, making me feel marginally better at seeing her.

Five years ago, I was both relieved and angry, justified and hurt, that I wasn't invited to her wedding. I wouldn't have gone anyway but I wanted to make that choice instead of having her make it for me. Especially when the entire town was invited to their nuptials.

There was a time when we had promised to be each other's maids of honor since we both had older brothers instead of sisters. Knowing I was missing out on her big day hurt even though the man she was meeting at the end of the aisle hurt a hell of a lot more.

But then, the wedding was called off. I heard from Mom that Anna ended it. No one knows why, or exactly what transpired between Anna and Sean. But they didn't marry or start a life together. To be honest, I don't know what either of them are up to now since I unfollowed or blocked them, and most of our old friend group, on social media.

I was in a nothing phase, with nothing left to give, and cutting ties with my past seemed like a healthy option. But now, they're both here tonight, and I wish I had a little insight into their current lives.

"Here you are," a man says, stepping up beside Anna. He passes her a champagne flute.

Anna smiles, her eyes radiating warmth, as she accepts the flute. She looks back to me. "Harper, this is my husband, George. George, this is—"

"Your childhood best friend." George's smile is wide, his tone sincere.

I shuffle back half a step, surprised by how pleased George looks to meet me. Damien's hand widens on my back, his thumb and pinkie both slipping beneath the silky material of my dress. His touch is grounding, reminding me that I've got this. That I'm okay.

Slowly, I extend a hand and paste a smile on my face. "It's nice to meet you, George." I clear my throat and dip my head. "It's good to see you again, Anna." The words surprise both of us. Anna's eyes widen and I nearly laugh because now that I've said them, I realize they're true. It is good to see her again. It's good that she's married and appears to be...happy.

Standing in our high-school gym, the space where we once whispered secrets and spent endless hours rehearsing dance routines, as adults, brings things full circle.

Our lives have moved on. We've grown up. By harboring hurt and hate from the past, the only thing I've done was stunt my own present. And for what? I moved back to Tennessee for my dream job in a city I love that's close to my family. Yet, I've done nothing to properly build a community here. I haven't sought out friendships, save for Leo and now Damien. I haven't invested my time or energy in building a home here.

That stops now.

Releasing an exhale, I turn into the unwavering wall of muscle at my back. "This is—"

Damien shifts, removing his hand from my back as his other hand curls around my hip. "Harper's boyfriend."

I bite down on my bottom lip, trying not to giggle. I know we said we'd do this as a fake couple, but hearing

Damien own the words out loud fills me with a lightness that feels a lot like laughter.

"Damien," I say, grinning up at him.

He smiles down at me, his eyes shining with pride. *We got this.*

I inch closer into his side as he shakes Anna's and George's hands.

"It's nice to meet you," Anna replies. "I hear you're living in the city now, Harper. How are you settling in?"

"Good," I say, meaning it. I briefly fill her in on my job with the Coyotes before asking about her work.

She dips her head, her eyes cutting to George. "I was working at The Teapot—"

"Ooh, I love it there," I admit, recalling the hours Anna and I used to spend walking through the aisles of different teas and tea-based products before collapsing in the comfy chairs, surrounded by a makeshift library, a ragtag collection of books, at the back.

"I know!" Anna squeals, her eyes bright. "But I left last year after our son was born."

"You're a mom," I breathe out, surprise and...genuine happiness filling my tone.

Anna nods. "His name is Eric, after—"

"Your dad. He must have loved that."

"Oh, he's a proud grandpa all right."

"That's wonderful, Anna," I say, meaning it. "I'm happy for you."

"Thanks, Harper. And I'm..." Her eyes cut to Damien before meeting mine again. "I'm happy you're home." Remorse colors her irises. "I'm sorry the way everything happened between us. Sorrier than you'll ever know."

I dip my head, silently accepting her apology. It feels good to hear it but not nearly as necessary as I once thought.

Instead, it's enough to see that her life has moved on and she's...herself.

"I never meant to hurt you," Anna's voice cracks.

Beside me, Damien draws George into a conversation that offers Anna and me a moment of privacy.

"I was jealous and bitter and..." She shakes her head. "You deserved better, Harper."

"Thank you." My voice cracks but some of the fissures in my heart snap back into place. "I appreciate your saying that."

"I should have said it years ago," she admits, gesturing around the gym. "And not here, at our ten-year reunion."

I shrug. "It's good to see you."

"You too." She holds my eyes for a moment before they dart to Damien and back again. "Wow," she mouths.

And I laugh, the moment feeling like an old memory. The instant connection a high-school girl shares with her best friend. A silent understanding, built on history and half-forgotten secrets. Nostalgia.

Anna grins. I smile back.

"See you around?" She tilts her head.

I nod. "See you around." I mean it too. Not that I'll actively seek her out, but I will be spending more time in our hometown. I will be reasserting my presence here.

She draws George away and I turn to face Damien.

"You did it," he murmurs.

I release a deep breath. "I did."

"How do you feel?"

"Like I could use a drink."

Damien laughs and steers me toward the makeshift bar. Dipping down, his lips brush the shell of my ear. "I'm proud of you, Henderson."

I glance at him over my shoulder. "For what?"

"You're gracious, babe. So damn purehearted."

"You're making everything tonight easier on me," I admit.

"Good." He flags down the bartender who indicates he'll be with us in a minute. "Champagne?" he asks me.

"Are we celebrating?"

"Mm-hmm." He nods.

I arch an eyebrow.

"Now that the most fearful part of your night is out of the way—"

"We haven't seen Sean yet."

Damien nods slowly, his eyes studying mine. "Why do I get the feeling that seeing Anna was more stressful?"

I shrug, not admitting that he's right. Anna's betrayal cut deeper than Sean's cheating. Losing Anna's friendship hurt more than losing Sean as a boyfriend.

"Still, you want to have some fun?" He tips his head toward the dance floor.

My mouth falls open. "You dance?"

"I should be on *Dancing with the* fucking *Stars*."

A laugh tumbles from my throat. Damien smirks.

"Two champagnes," I order.

When we have the flutes in hand, I take a greedy sip. All the nerves I've been experiencing, all the dread I've been harboring, about this evening melt away.

"I should warn you, I used to be captain of the dance team." I lean against the bar, watching Damien.

His eyes brighten playfully and I feel it—a spark—down to my core. "We could be the talk of your reunion," he muses, resting an elbow casually on the bar top. "I mean, if you want to fade into the background, I'm happy to do that. But if you want to remind everyone here exactly who Harper Henderson is, I'm game, babe."

A giggle drops from my mouth. A giggle I haven't heard since I stood among this same group of people my senior year of high school. We were getting ready to take the football field for graduation and I was high on the excitement of possibility. The future. College and friendships and being in love.

Those old feelings shouldn't surge right now but here they are, making me feel girlish and beautiful, softening my jaded edges and causing me to blush.

"You're trouble, Damien Barnes."

"You like it, Harper Henderson." He drains his flute and places it on the bar. Lifting an eyebrow, half in challenge, half in jest, he extends his hand.

I dip my flute back and drink all the bubbly before placing my hand in his.

"Let's dance," I say as he leads me to the center of the dance floor.

I smile and exchange hellos with former classmates. Friends. Girls from the dance team who grew into women, wives, and mothers, and professionals. Guys from my classes who transformed into class dads and dentists.

Damien spins me into his embrace and grips my hip, clasps my hand. Dropping me into a dip, he pulls me back up, eyes laughing, mouth grinning. He presses a fast kiss to my cheek. "Let's."

The tempo of the music changes and I hang on for the best dance of my life.

SIX

DAMIEN

DRUNK ON HARPER HENDERSON is the best buzz
I've ever had.

We dance, we drink, we chat and mingle and joke. And
I have a better time than anyone is supposed to at these
kinds of events.

"You've been back for a year now, Harper. Why don't
we ever see you?" a woman asks as Harper shows me the
restrooms.

Harper fumbles for a moment, her smile tightening as
the woman touches the crook of her elbow. "Hi, Mrs.
Collins," she says, turning to me. "This is Sean's mother.
She also helped plan tonight's event."

"I *did* plan it," Mrs. Collins emphasizes with a huff, her
eyes cutting over to Anna's mother, Mrs. Drew, who is deep
in conversation with Mrs. Riker.

I fight the urge to snicker. Or look around unimpressed.
Or—

Harper grips the back of my shirt.

I clear my throat. "Nice to meet you. I'm—"

"Damien Barnes," she interjects. "I know." Her gaze

sharpens, bouncing from Harper to me and back again. "Your mother never mentioned you're dating an *athlete*."

Harper pales slightly.

"That's my fault." I kiss Harper's temple. "I'm sure she will soon," I add, tucking Harper into my side. "I haven't had a chance to introduce Harper to my folks yet so we were waiting, you know, until we could both introduce our families. But I can't wait to meet your mom, love." I drop another kiss to the tip of her nose, laying it on thick.

"She's going to love you," Harper murmurs, amusement flashing in her eyes.

"I'll say," Mrs. Collins mutters.

"Good seeing you, Mrs. Collins," Harper says, making our getaway.

She escorts me to the bathroom, the two of us holding back our laughter until we clear the corner of the hallway and are out of view.

"Jesus, she's insufferable," I mutter.

Harper shakes her head. "I remember her being hard-headed but nothing like that. There was a time when she was like family to me."

I search her expression for a flash of regret, or sadness, but her face is clear, her voice strong. It eases something in my stomach—the realization that she's not pining away for this Sean guy like I imagined.

Like a part of me feared. Which is stupid, seeing as I'm her plus-one and she's just my neighbor. I shake off the weird feelings and indicate the men's room. "Thanks for the escort."

"Didn't want you to get lost."

"Or you didn't want to lose your buffer."

"That too." She gives a little wave as I dip into the bathroom.

When I'm washing my hands, a stall door opens, and Leo Quincy walks out. He's a tough dude to read and given his reputation—fast on the field, quiet off of it—and team, it's hard to know if he's just a nice guy or good at hiding more sinister qualities.

"You having fun?" he asks, flipping on the faucet.

"More than I thought I would," I admit.

"Yeah. You're here with Harper. She's good people."

I grab a paper towel and nod. "You know her well?"

He's quiet for a moment, studying me, before a smile moves over his face. "Whatever you're thinking, man, don't. I know Harper because she was always a nice girl, cool to chill with, and non-judgmental. Now that our paths cross at work, I can tell she hasn't changed much since high school. Eh, she might be funnier now."

I crack a grin, deciding Leo's an all right guy. "Harper and I, we're—"

He holds up a hand, cutting me off. "You don't owe me, or anyone, an explanation, Barnes. You and Harp do y'all."

"You here with anyone?"

He shakes his head and holds the door open for me. "I haven't had something real in a long, long time." He quiets as his eyes land, and hold, on a woman speaking with Harper.

"High school long?" I guess.

He nods. "Too long."

"Hey!" Harper looks up when she sees us. "I was just catching up with Tess."

A sophisticated-looking woman with blonde hair pulled into a low chignon smiles. Next to me, Leo stills. Tess's smile widens.

And I can't stop the chuckle that drops from my mouth.

Harper cuts me a look, that amusement I love flashing in her eyes.

"I'm glad you came, Leo," Tess says.

"Now, I am too," he replies.

Harper catches on and slips her arm through mine. "I want to show Damien some things from back in the day," she says, pulling me out of the hallway.

"You don't need to show me the hockey trophies, babe," I mutter in her ear as we slip into the main hallway. "I got my own."

Harper chuckles. "They would be the *football*, not hockey, trophies."

"Damn, cut me some slack. I'll make you a puck bunny yet."

Harper cuts me a look.

I grin. "But a classy one. Best dressed."

"Shut up," she laughs, hitting me in the stomach with the back of her hand. "They set up an area with different photos and memorabilia—nostalgia type shit—from our class."

"You must be real nostalgic," I comment.

She laughs again but stills when we come to an empty classroom. Peeking her head inside, her shoulders pinch together, and a half laugh bubbles up from her throat.

I slide my hand down Harper's arm, interlacing our fingers, and look into the classroom over her head. It's a science lab, set up with stations of sinks and Bunsen burners.

"Bad memories?" I ask.

"Bittersweet," she replies honestly, turning to stare at me. Her naked back rests along the doorjamb and I slip into the small space across from her, letting her floral scent wash over me. "I was happy in high school. I didn't have that awkward phase or question what I was meant to do with my life. Back then, all I wanted was to go away to college, have experiences, and come home to marry Sean. It was afterwards that..."

"That?"

"All the insecurities started." Her voice is nearly a whisper and I lean closer, reach out to touch her cheek, the side of her neck.

"You have nothing to be insecure about."

She arches an eyebrow, her eyes holding mine. The amusement from earlier is gone, filled with questioning and longing and that spark.

A heat I want to burn myself in.

My eyes drop to her mouth and the second her lips part, I'm on them, covering their softness with my want.

My hands wrap around her waist, drawing her closer, kissing her deeper. She moans as my tongue dips into her mouth, teasing hers.

"Damien..." Her voice is raw. Her eyes fly open, and she looks over my shoulder at the empty hallway. When she turns back to me, I pull away slightly. What the hell am I doing? I can't make out with her in an open hallway. "We're alone."

"Not a chance I'm willing to take," I bite out, taking her hand and pulling her into the science lab. I kick the door closed behind us.

The science lab is dark, only the moonlight streaming through the windows. It casts shadows on the long workbenches and gleams off the clusters of beakers and test tubes.

Turning Harper into me, I kiss her again, my hands finding the soft swells of her cheeks this time. She sinks into me, matching me kiss for kiss, her body pressed along mine.

When her hands untuck the back of my shirt and her fingers caress the skin of my back, I groan.

When was it last like this? Electric and needy?

Harper's hands flatten along my back, and I tug the hair at the nape of her neck, gaining more access to her mouth, her neck, the high, round curves of her breasts I want to taste.

She arches into me, silently asking for more. And I give it to her, my hand slipping under the skirt of her dress, my fingers teasing her over the satin of her panties. I back her up until she's leaning against the tallest workbench, her lower back cutting into the edge. I shift our position and slip my hand around her lower back so the countertop doesn't streak her skin with a red line.

She mewls and I swear, looking up to make sure we're still alone. The fact that anyone can walk in at any time, the high probability that her other classmates are wandering the halls, recalling memories from high school, on the other side of the door, heightens everything about this moment.

Harper's breathing is ragged, and I kiss her hard, swallowing her sounds as I shift her to a lower workbench. Lifting her, I place her on the edge of a counter and part her knees, stepping between her thighs and rolling up the material of her dress.

She watches me intently, rolling her lips together as vulnerability swims in her eyes. "I don't normally do this."

"Watch as a man gets you off?" I trail my fingers up the inside of her thigh. The growing wet patch on her panties turns me on just as much as the lust that clouds her eyes. Fuck, I want her to watch as I get her off.

"Revert to high-school fantasies," she admits.

I snort, cupping her, but stop to look up. "You fantasized about hooking up in the science lab?"

She bites the corner of her mouth, her cheeks blazing. "It was years ago."

"Go on."

"I used to fantasize about getting it on in here, the last place anyone would expect. I was captain of the dance team and hooked up with Sean under the bleachers. Or in the locker room. Never someplace smart like the lab or the library. It seemed...forbidden."

I growl, hating that she's said his name. That she's thinking of him in this moment, our moment. It's irrational and ridiculous because I'm just a plus-one, but I can't escape the jealousy that swims in my veins.

Instead, I ignore it and kiss her hard as my fingers push her panties to the side. I swipe along her slit, swallowing her moan, as my thumb applies pressure to her clit.

Tearing my lips away, I kiss down her neck, taste the floral fragrance she wears as I nip at her sensitive skin. Harper grasps the back of my head, holding my mouth against her skin as I quicken the pace of my fingers. She grinds against me, almost slipping off the counter as I sink one finger inside her. Harper pants, her skin flushing, as I bite the curve of her shoulder.

"Damien."

I look up, watching as her eyes close. I add a second finger, pumping slowly as emotion washes over her face.

"I got you, Harper," I encourage, quickening my pace. My cock twitches and my skin feels too tight as I watch her fall over the edge.

Harper convulses around my fingers and fuck if it's not the hottest thing I've ever experienced.

A loud bang, like a locker door closing, crashes on the other side of the lab. "Remember we had chemistry in here?" A loud laugh rings out.

Footsteps fill the hallway, broken conversations of old times drowning out our heavy breathing as Harper comes down from her orgasm and I try to simultaneously clean and cover her up. Fuck, I need to get my cock under control.

I twist Harper away from the door and know that if anyone cracks it open, I can pull her into a kiss and all anyone would see is her naked back because of her sexy dress.

I step out from between her thighs and push her knees together, taking up the space at her side so I can kiss her cheek.

Harper blinks slowly, a smile working its way over her gorgeous face. She reaches for me and I snicker, shaking my head as I step away.

Confusion rings her irises, a flare of vulnerability, and she fiddles with her nose ring. I move back into her space, wanting to put her mind at ease. I wrap an arm around her waist and drop my lips to her ear. "I want your hot hands on me more than I want to breathe, Harper."

She stills, waiting for me to continue.

"I want to take this further. Badly. But I don't want anyone to see us together like that. When you're with me, your moans and blushes are mine. If any man walked in, I'd fucking deck him."

She inhales sharply, giving a little nod of understanding.

"But fuck if I don't have the worst case of blue balls."

She chuckles. "Can I help?"

"Tell me something awful," I command.

"I had no idea you were a hockey player."

I chuckle. "That wasn't awful; that was truthful."

"I used to think your parents bought your penthouse for you," she tries again.

Christ, she's too fucking purehearted. "They could if they wanted to," I admit. "They gifted me my ride."

She shifts, sliding off the table and fixing her dress. She glances down at my dick and smirks.

"You surprise me, Damien Barnes."

The sincerity of her statement hits me square on, helping me get my raging desire for her under control. I don't know if it's good or bad, that my surprising her makes my chest feel tingly, makes me want to prove that I can somehow keep surprising her. "Is that good or bad?"

She holds my gaze for a beat, her eyes serious. "Good, I think."

I grin, tucking a strand of hair behind her ear. "I think you're pretty great, Harper Henderson." Then, I kiss her once on the mouth. "Come on, let's go dance and let your classmates make up rumors about us."

She laughs, lets me take her hand and guide her back to the gym. Before we make it, a man steps into the hallway and Harper's footsteps falter.

He narrows his eyes, giving me a dirty look, before staring at her.

"Harper," his voice cuts through the hallway, an edge of possessiveness I don't like in his tone.

Harper halts. "Hi, Sean."

Fuck.

SEVEN
HARPER

SEAN COLLINS DOESN'T LOOK NEARLY AS hideous as I'd hoped. But he doesn't look half as good as Damien either. I know it's petty as hell but...Damien Barnes is a ten to Sean's measly six point five.

I'm taking that as a win.

As I study my high school's former star quarterback, I'm relieved that the wave of pain I anticipate doesn't come. At least, not as a wave; it's more like stepping into a shallow puddle.

"You look good," Sean says. His eyes scan my body, narrowing when they land on Damien's hold on my hip.

Keeping one arm wrapped around me, Damien extends his other hand. "She looks gorgeous, doesn't she?" His voice is calm, almost aloof, but I feel the tension in his hold. "I'm Damien, Harper's boyfriend."

Boyfriend, not date. Label, not ambiguity.

The feel of his mouth on mine, just minutes ago, rolls through my mind and I shiver.

"Sean Collins." Sean shakes Damien's hand and clears his throat. "Hockey, right?"

"The Thunderbolts," Damien replies easily.

"Yeah," Sean mutters, scratching the back of his neck. "Haven't seen you since you moved back," he says to me.

I shrug, leaning into Damien's touch. I open my mouth to give a generic response when Damien cuts in—

"That's my fault." He presses a kiss to the crown of my head. "I travel a lot and when I'm here, I try to keep Harper all to myself."

Something I can't fully read, although it looks a lot like remorse, flashes through Sean's eyes. It dulls the sting of seeing him again but doesn't fill me with the triumphant vibes I anticipated.

Sean grunts in response, looking away.

"How've you been?" I ask, way gushier than I would have thought myself capable of.

"Fine," Sean says.

"Are you still working for your father?" I try again.

Sean nods. "Yeah. We're working together."

Sean's dad owns a custom carpentry shop and taught Sean everything he knows at a young age. Sean's plan was always to go pro for football but an injury his freshman year of college sidelined those dreams. "That's wonderful, Sean. I know your dad was always very proud of you."

At my words, Sean's stare intensifies. The corner of his mouth pulls upward, and he shuffles his feet. "Thanks, Harp. That means a lot. You know, I'm sure he'd love to see you. If you're ever in the neighborhood, stop by. You were always the daughter he never had." He dips his head. "Even after."

My throat tightens. While Sean's mother and I got along, we didn't have the special bond his father and I shared.

Damien's grip on my hip tightens. I glance up at him and notice the tick in his jaw.

"Thanks. Yeah. Um, tell him I was asking about him," I manage, wondering if part of the reason Sean and Anna's relationship fell apart was because of Mr. Collins' disapproval.

"He'll love that." Sean smirks.

I smile. "It was good to see you."

"You too, Harper. Take care of yourself." His eyes make one more pass down my body. "I really hope to see you again."

What? My smile slips as I definitely wasn't expecting that. Does he mean it as a casual quip? Or does he truly mean it? Does Sean still think about me?

Confusion rocks through me as I only ever considered the heartache of seeing Sean again. I never thought he'd regret losing me. Or want me back.

Damien seems to expand behind me, his muscles hardening, his body locking down. The hallway shrinks, the little bubble between Sean, Damien, and me bursting.

Sean reaches out and runs a finger down my forearm, his touch lingering on the back of my hand. "Glad you came tonight, Harper."

A rumble works its way through Damien's chest. Did he just growl? I tear my eyes away from Sean and glance up at Damien, frowning when he won't meet my eyes.

Shaking my head, I ball my fingers into a fist to knock off Sean's touch. "You too. Have a good night, Sean."

Stepping forward, I link my fingers with Damien's and give them a squeeze as we re-enter the gym and have another drink.

As the alcohol rolls through my bloodstream, I slowly relax and enjoy the remainder of the evening. Now that I've conversed with Anna and Sean, the stress of tonight melts away. Instead, I turn my focus on Damien and the exceptional fake boyfriend he's morphed into.

We dance, we mingle, we laugh. But every time Sean enters our line of sight, Damien bristles. And when he kisses me good night at my doorstep, his mouth holds a possessive edge that didn't exist before.

Trying not to read into it but unable to let tonight and all it's wonderful surprises go, I send him a text before bed.

Me: Thanks for a great night, Damien. I like surprises.

A moment later, a text comes through. My smile drops when I read it.

Unknown: Harper, it was great seeing you tonight. I'm taking a chance and hoping you haven't changed your number. Now that you're back in town for good, it's a sign. I'd love to see you. Make amends and prove that I've changed. Prove that our paths were supposed to cross again. Sleep well.

Sean? It has to be because who else would write that message?

To be petty, I tap out a reply.

Me: Who is this?

Then, I drift off to sleep with a smile on my face.

———

BUT WHEN I wake up the next morning and read my messages, my smile is long gone. Instead, a ball of frustration dipped in hurt rolls through me.

Sean Collins: It's Sean. Do you have plans this week? Dinner Wednesday night?

I delete that right away because...seriously? He just met my "boyfriend" and he's trying to take me to dinner?

Damien: Yo, buddy! You awake? Breakfast?

Buddy? After what happened last night...

I drag myself from bed and ignore Damien as I take a shower. I mean, I ignore his message, but thoughts of him flood my mind.

Last night was...unexpected. It was hot and intense, and I was so freaking breathless.

But it was also fun and thrilling and passionate.

So, we kissed. He got me off. That doesn't mean more than what it was, right? The past couple weeks that Damien and I have hung out, there hasn't been any blurred lines or inappropriate touching. We're friends who...what? Help each other out? Sometimes cross a line?

My stomach grumbles and as much as I know accepting his invite for breakfast will only confuse me more, I *am* hungry.

Turning off the shower, I wrap a towel around my body before twisting my hair up into a smaller, matching towel.

I walk into my bedroom to answer Damien's message when there's knock on my door.

Sighing, I move to the door and pull it open.

Damien greets me, his arm braced over his head on the doorjamb, a scowl on his face.

"This is how you open the door?" He widens his eyes.

I shrug, turning back toward my bedroom. He follows me inside.

"You didn't even check if you knew me," he presses.

"Who else would knock on my door this early on a Sunday morning?"

"It's nearly noon."

I glance at him over my shoulder, wagging my eyebrows. "I was busy last night."

His eyes snap to mine when he realizes I just caught him checking me, no, my ass, out. "Har, har."

"Let me get dressed real quick. Then, I'd love to grab a bite, friend."

He rocks back, surprised at my word choice. But my tone was even, normal, and for that I'm grateful. It's obvious that last night was just a moment between Damien and me. We were both caught up in it, probably me more, given that I saw Sean and Anna for the first time in years. Plus, I hadn't hooked up with a guy in months and had been wracked with nerves about the reunion for weeks.

Clearly, I needed a release, an outlet. And everyone knows sexual releases are the best kind.

Yeah...keep telling yourself that.

Shrugging out of my towel, I tug on a clean pair of panties, roll my eyes at the bra hanging from my bathroom doorknob, and shimmy into a long, cutout, maxi dress. It's breezy, comfortable, and the perfect choice after spending a night wrapped in a skintight little number meant to entice.

Entice it did because...exhibit A, Damien Barnes.

But that was last night and today we're back to us. Friends. *Neighbors.*

That's all we'll ever be.

I tie my hair in a loose braid that flops over one shoulder, slip into sandals, and grab my purse.

"I'm ready," I announce, waltzing back into the living room.

Damien looks up from the framed family photo he's holding. He places it back on the coffee table, his eyes swinging around my space. We usually hang at his penthouse, and this is the first time he's been in my home. "You have a brother."

"I do. Kellan. He's in the Air Force, stationed in Florida."

"Oh. Well, I'm surprised I didn't meet your parents last night."

"I made my mom promise *not* to volunteer. It would have been too much."

"Her meeting me? Parents love me."

"I don't doubt that. But no, I mean, her and Anna and Sean and Sean's mom all in the same place..." I shiver at the idea of more drama and make a face. "Besides, last night is now done and over. In the past. I am so ready to move on, greet my future."

Damien pauses, his eyes skating over me. After a moment, the aloofness he usually wears slips back into place and he smirks. "This future includes coffee, right?"

"Iced and sweet," I confirm.

"Let's do it." He holds my apartment door open for me and we both slip outside.

In the morning light, there's no hand holding. There's no mention of the passionate kisses we exchanged last night. Or the way he got me off faster than any man I've been with since college.

Instead, we settle back into our respective roles: friendly neighbors with a budding friendship. A friendship that allows for an occasional plus-one/fake date/stand-in significant other.

If I'm being honest with myself, it's the best of both worlds.

But I've always hated being honest with myself.

———

"OPEN UP," Damien calls out, his knock growing impatient.

"Jeez," I grumble, dragging myself to unlock the front door.

He frowns when he sees me. "You're already sleeping?"

I squint at the clock on my living room wall. "It's almost eleven."

"You're not even thirty, no wonder you're alone."

I roll my eyes. "What do you want?"

Damien strides into my place, kicking the door closed behind him. He places a brown paper bag on the kitchen island. "I'm bored."

"This is my problem how?"

"I'm here to hang out."

I groan but inside, my heart rate ticks up. Even though I'm exhausted, we both know I won't tell him to leave. Partly because we're friends. And partly because...we're not *only* friends.

"Your staying is contingent on what's in the bag."

Damien snickers. "Then I'm pretty sure I can move in."

My eyes widen when I read the logo on the paper bag. "You got me a buttermilk pie from Annabelle's?"

"You're welcome," Damien says as I open the bag and moan.

"You have to wait in line for hours for these."

"Trust me, I know." He opens my fridge and pulls out a bottle of white wine we opened earlier in the week. Then, he grabs two wine glasses. His familiarity with my kitchen, his confidence of his place in my life...it's new but it doesn't feel new. It feels like Damien and I have known each other a lot longer than one month.

"Admit it. You love me," I deadpan.

He glances over his shoulder and smirks. "You're tough

not to love, Harper."

Swoon. My heart rate triples at his words. Too bad he doesn't mean them.

I dip my head in agreement and silently accept the wine glass he holds out. Taking a sip, I relish the crisp pinot grigio before getting some plates, forks, and a pie cutter.

We sit at my kitchen table, and I cut us two thick slices of the best pie in Tennessee.

I moan as I bite into the flaky crust. "This is amazing."

"Yeah," he agrees, his eyes on me. "It sure is."

Again, I feel like he's saying more than he's letting on. I pause, my fork hovering over my plate as I hold his gaze. Something is amiss. Why the hell would Damien show up at this time with pie, pour me wine, and say half-truths? "What's going on?"

He leans back in his chair, drawing one arm over the back. "Nothing."

"Nope." I shake my head, pointing my fork at him. "You want something."

He licks his bottom lip, his eyes dropping to my chest before meeting my eyes again. "I want a lot of things, Harper."

I snicker and roll my eyes. "You want something *else*."

He grumbles something that sounds a lot like *losing my touch*. I grin, waiting him out.

"I need a favor," he says finally.

"What kind of favor?"

"One that I would do for you in a heartbeat."

"Hmm..." I lift my eyebrows.

He swears and clears his throat. "I need a date."

I smile. "A date?"

"To my parents' thirty-fifth wedding anniversary party."

I whistle, the sound low.

Damien rolls his eyes. "It's in Connecticut, at my parents' house, the last weekend of July."

"And you want to take me?" I question, thinking this over.

"Who else would I take?"

I shrug, secretly liking that he's not seeing another woman. I mean, he's not seeing me either but...he's hanging out with me more than anyone else. Ugh, does this make me pathetic? Damien Barnes and I are nothing except neighbors with a penchant for late-night drinks and mixed signals.

"Harper."

I look up, place my fork down.

"Will you please come with me to my parents' anniversary dinner?"

Knowing I can't say no, not after everything Damien did for me, I nod. "As your..."

"As my Harper," he says like it's perfectly clear.

I snort. "What's that mean?"

"You know, you're my friend, girl. Friend-girl."

I laugh even harder now. "Okay. Whatever. I'll go."

He grins, I smile, and we eat more pie.

Afterwards, snuggled up on my couch, watching *Peaky Blinders*, the weight of what I agreed to settles over me.

Do I want to meet Damien's parents? Will they like me? Will they want someone like me to date their son?

The questions make me uncomfortable because truth be told, I don't think I'm the woman they envision when they think of Damien's future. If everything he's told me is true—about his old money, Connecticut upbringing—I doubt my nose ring and snarky jokes are going to go over well.

My phone buzzes and I grin when I see my brother's face flash on the screen.

"It's my brother," I explain, swiping to answer. Damien pauses the episode. "Hey, Kel!"

"Miss your face, Harp," Kellan says the second we connect.

"You should call me more."

He snickers. "You should pick up when I call."

"Fair," I agree, since I haven't returned his last two calls.

"I want to know how the showdown went." My brother wags his eyebrows.

"The showdown?"

Damien straightens in his seat, looking at me curiously.

"Mom said you brought, and I quote, a 'sexy, hot hockey player' to your reunion," Kellan explains, using air quotes.

I crack up, turning the phone toward Damien. "Here's the sexy and hot man of the hour."

Damien looks startled but waves at my brother.

"What's up, man? Nice to meet you," Kellan says in the easygoing way of his.

I turn the phone screen back toward me and my brother gives me a look, flipping me the middle finger for putting him on the spot like that. I laugh harder.

"Good to meet you, too," Damien calls out.

Kellan chuckles. "You had fun?"

I nod.

"You shut down the dickhead?"

Damien laughs and I nod again.

Kellan grins. "Good. Happy for you, Harp. I won't keep you since you have, ahem, *company*, but call me this weekend."

"I will. I want to hear about your date with the 'stunning, level-headed flight attendant.'" I use air quotes around Mom's description of Kellan's most recent date.

Kellen groans. "This is why you need to answer my

calls. We can't have Mom being the messenger between us."

"I'll call you this weekend," I promise. "Love you, Kel."

"You too, Harp. Later."

I disconnect the call and place my phone down.

Damien glances over me, his expression thoughtful. He pulls my feet on his lap and casually massages my foot.

It's the kind of thing a boyfriend would do. It's the kind of easy connection I haven't had with a man since Sean.

And it's not even real. How depressing.

"You and your brother are close," he comments.

I smile at him. "Yeah. Kellan likes to pretend I'm a pain in the ass but he doesn't mean it. He calls me at least twice a week."

"And you don't answer?"

I shake my head. "Just the past few weeks have been busy. But normally, I always pick up. We talk a lot, otherwise Mom starts spinning stories..."

Damien chuckles and shakes his head like he doesn't know what to make of that. Before I can push him further, he restarts the episode.

Focusing on the TV show, I get lost in the world of 1920s Birmingham. A second episode starts and slowly, my eyes flutter closed, as I drift off to sleep. The last thing I remember is my head meeting a soft pillow, the weight of a thick blanket settling over me, and the sweetest press of a kiss to my forehead.

"Damien?"

"Sleep now, Harp. I'll see you in the morning."

"'Kay. Good night."

"Night, sweet girl."

Sweet girl? The term of endearment makes me smile because I'm more sour than sweet.

But I like that Damien thinks of me that way.

EIGHT

DAMIEN

"YOU'RE BRINGING HER HOME?" Cole sounds more impressed than surprised.

Axel Daire hides his gruff snicker behind a sip of his beer while his daughter, Lola, stares at me like I just announced I'm an amoeba.

"She's helping me out. That's it," I say.

"She's helping you out all right," Lola quips.

Beau snorts into his beer.

Axel shoots her a look. She rolls her eyes and huffs, excusing herself from the table.

Cole, Brawler, Beau, and I are hanging out, shooting the shit at Brawler's place. It's forty minutes outside the city so while Cole and Axel have caught up a few times, with Beau joining them when he's out this way visiting his gran and sister Bea, I've mostly missed out. Mainly because the thought of driving all this way wasn't intriguing enough.

That, and I have Harper just one floor down. Why would I trek out to the middle of nowhere when I could hang on Harper's couch and watch her reactions to season three of our show, *Peaky Blinders*.

Our show. I shake the thought from my head.

"You like her," Beau states quietly.

I look up, slide my beer between my two palms, and nod. "Yeah, I like her."

"You want your family to like her?" he presses.

I shrug but...fuck, is my collar tight? "Well, yeah, I wouldn't bring anyone home in the hopes that my family *not* like them."

Cole snickers.

"You know what he means," Axel bites out.

"We're just...friends." The excuse sounds lame even to me. "I mentioned Harper in passing to my dad and he pressed, telling me to bring her to the party. That and my brother Charlie..." I trail off, flicking a dismissive hand.

The guys stay quiet, waiting for me to continue. I don't talk about real things often, and never my family.

I sigh. "Charlie's got some shit going on. If I show up with a girl—"

"Friend," Beau says. "Practice saying it out loud. *Girlfriend.*"

Cole laughs and even Axel cracks a grin.

I flip him off and he chuckles, taking a swig of his beer.

"Anyway," I continue, "it takes some pressure, some attention, off Charlie."

"Fair," Axel says. "You want to keep it that way? The 'just friends' part?" he asks, curious.

"Why? You think bringing her home will mess things up between us?" It's a stupid question to ask since hell yeah, it will probably mess shit up between us.

Mom is going to hound her for information about her charitable causes and the designers she likes best. Charlie is going to go off the rails, hoping Harper's presence provides him with a cover. And Fiona...I have no idea how my sister will react. She's been more closed-off than usual lately. Withdrawn.

I slipped up when I mentioned Harper to Dad. His genuine happiness over my spending time with a woman, his outright asking me to invite her to his anniversary party, was a request I couldn't refuse.

Now, I'm taking the woman I like best to a pit full of vipers. It's more than a fucking mistake; it's a dead end.

"No." Beau's response to the question I asked Axel surprises me. "I don't think it will mess things up, but I do think it will change things between y'all."

Cole nods. "Beau's right. You either gotta go in with the understanding that you're friends, and nothing else. Or you have to go in and introduce her as the woman in your life."

Axel points his beer bottle at Cole. "Rookie knows what's up."

While they make a valid point, I shake my head. "Nah, it's not like that with Harp and me. We're cool, casual. Things between us are fun. They're easygoing and chill. We don't need a label, or a box, one way or the other." I shake my head. "Besides, if my mom truly thinks Harper's the woman of my dreams, she'll meddle too damn much."

Axel stares at me like I'm the dumbest motherfucker alive.

Beau's look is evened out with a quiet kind of understanding.

Even Cole, cinnamon roll Cole having experienced his first love just this past season, looks at me with a glimmer of pity in his expression.

I swear. "You guys don't get it. Harper and I, we're cool. She's helping me out the same way I stepped up for her at her reunion."

"Right," Axel scoffs. "And that night didn't confuse shit between you?"

"That night didn't make you feel comfortable asking her to *meet your family*," Beau tacks on.

Considering I didn't say peep about hooking up with Harper that night, I'm not surprised Axel read the situation correctly. "Your daddy senses are creepy."

"You saying 'daddy' is fucking creepy," he mutters.

Cole grins, Beau snorts, and I chuckle.

"All I'm saying is, figure out what you want, Barnes. What do you want with Harper? What do you want this to be?" Axel lifts an eyebrow before taking a swig of his beer. "If it's just a fun way to pass the summer, cool. Say that. Make sure she knows it. If there's potential for more, make sure she knows that too. Nothing fucking worse than blind-siding a woman. It hurts more than when it happens to you."

"It's the fucking worst," Beau agrees, the pain lacing his words nodding to a firsthand experience.

Cole nods in agreement.

"He's right!" Lola calls out from somewhere in the house.

Axel swears. "I thought you were going out?"

Lola laughs. "Jas is working and the four of you gossiping like old maids is more amusing."

"She's got a point," Cole agrees.

Axel shakes his head and grabs us another round of beers. "I hate when she's right."

I do too but this time, they're wrong.

I'm not going to blindside Harper. There's nothing for her to be off guard about. We're...more than friends. Doing our thing. We both know there's more between us than a friendly neighbor vibe. But we haven't crossed any serious lines we can't come back from. Unless the weekend with my family goes completely sideways. And while that's a possibility, it shouldn't ruin shit between us because we're not *together together*. There's respect there, mutual understanding, consideration and compassion.

I'm not going to hurt her. The thought alone tears me up inside and I realize that Axel is right about one thing: blindsiding Harper would be a hell of a lot worse than being blindsided by her. Because her hurting cuts deeper than my own pain.

ALL THOUGHTS of mutual understanding die a quick death when Leo Quincy answers Harper's door the following day.

"Hey, man," he says casually, tipping his head for me to enter.

I know they're friends. I know they work together. I know they've known each other for years. I know all that and still, jealousy washes over me like a tidal wave. It surges up from my stomach, clogs my throat, and sours the taste on my tongue.

What the fuck is he doing here? And why isn't he wearing a goddamn shirt?

"Want a smoothie?" he asks, picking up a blender and pouring out three smoothies. "Harp's in the shower but she'll be out any minute."

In the shower? Why the hell is she showering?

At the glower I'm directing at him, Leo chuckles. "Relax. We went for a run." He moves around the counter and reaches into a backpack. He pulls out a clean T-shirt and slides it on.

"A run?" I question, sounding skeptical and pissed off and...fucking jealous.

"Harper told me you're bringing her home to meet the parents." Leo settles back against the countertop and takes a sip of his smoothie. "That's big."

"It's casual," I retort, begrudgingly picking up the smoothie he poured for me. I take a drink and my anger doubles when it's fucking good.

"Yeah," he agrees. "That's what Harper said too."

I look up sharply. Leo meets my gaze but doesn't say anything, just takes a long pull of his smoothie.

The water in Harper's bathroom turns off.

The tension between Leo and me increases. Except the jealousy from a few seconds ago has diffused and instead, I get the feeling that he's not impressed with my taking Harper to my parents' anniversary party.

"Harper and I, we have an understanding," I explain.

Leo lifts his glass in my direction. "Man, whatever y'all decide."

I frown. His response should ease some of the tension filling my veins; instead, it thickens it. Why do I feel the need to explain myself to Leo?

To anyone?

"You hungry?" Harper asks as she exits her bedroom, using a towel to dry her damp hair.

She's fully dressed, rocking a pair of leggings and a crop top, and I breathe a sigh of relief. Thank God she didn't come out in a robe or worse, a towel.

"Hey, Damien!" she exclaims when she sees me, her smile wide.

I relax, smirking back. "What are you up to?"

"Leo and I just went for a run," she explains, boosting herself up to sit on the countertop next to Leo. He hands her a smoothie, and she takes a big gulp. "Thanks, Leo. This is delish."

They're easy around each other. There are no surreptitious glances. No fleeting touches. It's just friendship and it's obvious.

Jesus, what is wrong with me? Why am I overthinking everything with Harper?

Leo drains his smoothie and places the glass in the sink. "I'm gonna take off."

"You don't want to eat?" Harper asks.

Leo dips his head. Is he fucking blushing? He shuffles his weight from one foot to the next. "I asked Tess if she wanted to grab a bite and..." He pulls his phone out of his pocket and shakes it. "We're going to meet up in a bit."

"Awww." Harper places a hand over her heart, looking genuinely excited about this news. "I love this, Leo." She hops down from the countertop and slings an arm around Leo's waist. "Let me know how it goes."

"Yeah. You wanna run tomorrow?" he asks, slapping my shoulder in farewell as Harper walks him to the door.

"Sure. I have a ten AM meeting I need to be in the office for. Can we meet at six?" Harper pulls open the door.

"Yeah. See you later, Harp. Barnes."

"Have a great lunch," Harper says.

"Later." I lift a hand.

Harper closes the door after Leo and turns toward me. "You hungry?"

My gaze skates over her, taking in the way the leggings hug her curves. The little dip as her waist gives way to her hips. Her taut tummy and the flash of a pink bra underneath her white crop top. Yeah, I'm fucking hungry.

"Starving," I admit.

"Cool." Harper swipes up her phone. "Sushi?"

"Okay."

She punches in an order and it's casual. Familiar. Kind of like how she was interacting with Leo.

Does she see me the same?

The thought unsettles me because I want her to see me as...more. More invested in her, more involved in her life.

She drops down her phone and resumes her perch on the countertop. "It will be here in forty."

"Great." I clear my throat. "How's your week been?"

I slide onto a barstool to her right, angling it so I can see her better.

"Busy," she sighs. "I'm glad it's the weekend. Not that I have many friends in town, and the few I do have are all guys"—she wrinkles her nose and I realize she misses having girl friends—"but there's been more social gatherings with the Coyotes back in town for preseason. Plus, things are gearing up at the office. Your parents' party will be my last weekend of total freedom so"—she smirks—"make it a good one for me."

I snort. "You have any doubts?"

Her eyes hold mine, a flare of something I can't read sparking in their depths. "No, no doubts."

"My dad's looking forward to meeting you," I admit. "I confirmed last night that you're coming with."

"As..."

I roll my lips together. Do I want to introduce Harper as my girl or my date? Do I want my family to take an vested interest in her? Or is it better if she just exchanges small talk with Fiona and talks football with Charlie?

There's no doubt she can handle my family in the moment; I know she can hold her own. But what about afterwards? When all Mom's snippy comments have had time to marinate in her head? When Charlie's sunny personality gives way to cutting words due to drugs or alcohol? Will she stick around? Or will she cut ties like Brittney, the last girl I introduced to my family over a decade ago. I look at Harper, read the hesitant hope in her gaze. My heart thuds, pulsing in my eardrums. The last thing I want is to hurt her. I can handle this weekend, right? I can balance Harper and the Barnes Family. I can avoid the bullshit drama.

I exhale slowly. "My girlfriend. Come as my girlfriend."

"Your *fake* girlfriend..." she says slowly.

I shrug, wanting to refute her word choice but unable to form the words. "We're friends, Harper."

"Who sometimes hook up."

I nod.

Hurt ripples through her eyes and I shift closer to her, wrapping a hand around the back of her knee. Fuck, am I going to hurt her no matter what I decide? No matter which way this thing we're doing pans out? "I'm not seeing anyone else."

"You can; we're *just* friends."

The fact that she doesn't respond with a "me neither" bothers me. Is she casually dating? Or thinking about it? Especially since all her friends are guys? Does she want to date?

I squeeze the back of her leg. "I don't want to."

She narrows her eyes at me.

"Look, I've never been in a real, adult relationship before. Only had one girlfriend my whole life and that was in high school."

Her eyes widen in surprise and her lips part. "Seriously?"

I nod.

"Why not?" she presses.

At her questioning, my stomach knots. I start to shrug it off, but she keeps talking.

"I mean, your parents are celebrating thirty-five years. Isn't their marriage a good one?"

"Yeah." I slide my hand down to her ankle, still holding on. "But my family isn't like yours, Harper."

"Meaning?"

I blow out a sigh. "There are expectations. There are rules to abide by. My pursuing hockey broke the first rule."

Surprise ripples over her face. "Which is?"

"I should have followed in my father's, in Charlie's, footsteps."

"But surely they're proud of you. I mean, look at all you achieved. You're an NHL player."

"Yeah," I laugh, dipping my head. "In my world, the one I was brought up in, I should have become a surgeon. Or a hedge fund manager. I should marry a socialite with a last name that has as much purchasing power as mine. I should be consumed with building a network and forging connections that grow my family's wealth and status. And...I'm not."

"What about your siblings?"

I sigh. "Charlie's all right. I used to idolize him, and I guess a part of me misses that. He's been struggling since his fiancée cheated on him."

Harper blanches.

"Now, he's partying way too hard. He's a few months out of forcing my parents' intervention."

"And your sister? You have a nephew, right?"

I grin, thinking of Garrett. "Yeah, Garrett is the shit. But something is going on with my sister. She hasn't been herself lately. Look, coming home with me is a bit like being fed to the vipers." I pause, studying Harper's expression.

She grins, shaking her head. She doesn't look concerned at all.

"I don't want to scare you off," I whisper my deepest fear.

Her eyes soften and she shifts closer to me. "Impossible."

"You haven't met the Barnes family."

"I don't need to; I met *you*."

Her words soothe something deep inside, offering some relief about my concerns surrounding this party. "The expectations my family has for me, they're not the kind I'd ever bring a woman I care about into."

Harper frowns. "It's illegal?"

"No," I chuckle, shaking my head. "It's soul-less. You'll see when you come to my family home. You're too damn pure for the Barneses, Harper."

She reaches out and cups my cheek. A small smile curls her lips, and I can tell she doesn't fully believe me. She doesn't fully understand.

"They're wealthy, Harper. My family is really wealthy."

"I know; I've seen your car."

I chuckle. "The way I grew up...it's what you see in those movies, television shows like *Gossip Girl*."

She leans forward, her elbows dropping to her knees. Her eyebrows dip as awareness begins to dawn. "Seriously?"

"Yes. And look, I know my parents love me, I know they want me to settle down, but my lifestyle—"

"Which is?"

"Hockey, being on the road with the team, always antic-ipating a trade...that lifestyle is one they don't understand. Or, to be honest, respect."

"You really don't think they're proud of you?" A ripple

of hurt, hurt for me, rounds out her words. It's thoughtful and empathetic. I close my eyes for a beat, soaking it in.

I grip her ankle tighter. "Not the way yours are. They're not supportive the way your parents are. My siblings and I don't have an easy understanding the way you and Kellan do."

"I, wow, Damien, I had no idea."

"That's my fault. I don't talk about them a lot."

Harper shakes her head. "I like you, Damien. A lot. I want to understand you."

I smile. "I like you too, Henderson." I tug on her ankle, pulling her off the countertop and into my lap. "I like you a lot more than I've ever liked a woman before."

"Even the girl from high school?"

I laugh. "Even Brittney."

She peers up at me, wrapping one arm around my neck. "Is that good or bad?"

"Both," I admit honestly, kissing the tip of her nose. "I don't know what to do with it. With you."

"What do you want to do with me, Damien?" she asks coyly.

"A lot more than I should." My voice is lower than it was a moment ago. My gaze falls to her mouth and fucking hell her lips are soft. Plump. Kissable.

"Why shouldn't you?" she whispers, her eyes flaring.

"Because the last thing I want to do is hurt you, Harper. And a guy like me, with my family and my career and my lack of experience...that's the reality of it. I won't *not* mess this up. And with you, I care too fucking much to risk that."

"So..." She lets out a heavy exhale. "I'm your fake girlfriend."

I nod slowly. "This, this *thing* we've got going on, is the realest it's ever been for me."

She sighs, her eyes closing for a beat. She looks so peaceful, so beautiful and serene and *patient*, that my heart aches for her.

"I wish I could be more for you, Harp," I admit, my words thick. "But I won't ever be enough."

"I like you the way you are, Damien." She opens her eyes. "And I don't know if that's a good or bad thing. Because I'm not going to change who I am to fit into a man's life or family again."

"You shouldn't. Don't ever settle." I lift a hand to her cheek, brushing her hair back from her face. Her cheek presses into my palm and slowly, I lower my face to hers. She doesn't pull back. She barely breathes.

Right before my lips brush over hers, a knock sounds on the door and we both jump, our noses bumping.

"Shit, sorry," I say, brushing a finger down the slope of her nose.

She shakes her head and slides from my lap. "It's okay; I'm fine." She moves toward the door. "That's the sushi."

"Right," I agree, standing up.

The moment burns out like a candle. First it flickers, then it dims, then it's done.

I don't ever want to be done with Harper, but we can't exist in dimness forever.

NINE

HARPER

"HOW WAS LUNCH WITH TESS?" It comes out as a half gasp since Leo and I are on mile number four and while I always considered myself a runner, my performance pales in comparison to Leo. "How come you're not wheezing like me?"

Leo chuckles, the sound normal. Like he doesn't have an elevated heart rate and isn't pushing his body in the slightest. Damn running backs. "This is a warm-up for me, Harp."

"Came a long way since high school."

He snorts. "Nah, I still like robots."

Laughing, I come to a stop and drop my hands to my knees to catch my breath. When I stand, I heave out an exhale. Leo waits next to me, his hands interlaced behind his head. "You don't have to stop on my account."

He shrugs. "No offense, but this really is my warm-up. I've got a lift in a few hours."

I flip him the middle finger and he snickers.

"And I wanted to ask you about Tess anyway."

I straighten. "What about?"

"I like her. I've liked her since high school."

"Yeah. She's awesome."

"She's busy."

"Okay." I start to walk, and Leo falls into step beside me. "So are you."

"Exactly," he sighs. "Between her being a badass lawyer and me playing football, our last two dates fell through."

I wrinkle my nose. "That sucks."

"Yeah, but the season hasn't started yet, Harp. I feel like this is my chance to shoot my shot with her."

"So, shoot it."

"I'm trying but we're casual, you know? It's new. We're not exclusive or anything and..."

"And football season is starting."

"I'll be on the road a lot."

I sigh. "I hear you, Leo. It's not easy."

"Being an athlete?" he laughs.

I shoot him a grin. "Dating one. Hell, dating in general."

"Facts."

"Don't give up just yet. You guys need to carve out time for one another. It doesn't have to be a date or a dinner or something fancy. It can be a morning run or a smoothie or whatever you both can squeeze into your schedules. Just, prioritize time instead of trying to make it perfect."

He ponders that as we pause outside the smoothie bar we've come to frequent.

I wiggle my eyebrows and Leo snorts, pulling open the door. "We need to stop buying these. I can make them better."

"You signed a massive contract; you can splurge on a smoothie every now and then."

Leo laughs. "What's going on with you and Damien?"

"We leave for his parents' this weekend."

"You nervous?"

I wave to the barista. "Two green smoothies, please." Turning to Leo, I cross my arms over my chest. "Why would I be nervous?"

He gives me a look. "Meeting the family is a pretty big step. And it's a family event, not a casual lunch."

"Yeah, but I'm his fake friend-girl," I remind him, ignoring the fissure of pain that radiates from my heart at the reminder. What the hell is a friend-girl?

I've told Damien that I trust him, and I thought he trusts me too. Doesn't he realize that I've got his back and won't let him down? That I'll do whatever he needs me to do this weekend, the same way he showed up for me at my reunion?

Leo taps his Apple Watch for payment before I can pull up my card and I roll my eyes.

"You don't have to buy my smoothie."

"What?" He shrugs, shooting me a dimpled grin. "I signed a contract; I can afford it."

I laugh. "I didn't mean it like that."

"I know. Now, be honest. Do you really believe that's all y'all are?"

Pulling open the door and stepping back into the hot morning air, I shrug. "I don't know. It's...complicated."

"Dating's not easy," Leo reminds me.

I laugh again, drinking some of my smoothie. "I'm a little nervous," I admit. "Damien is from this other world. Old money, society type shit. And I'm..." I gesture to my nose ring.

Leo lifts an eyebrow. "A gorgeous, intelligent, hustling woman?"

I sigh. "In another stratosphere."

Leo shakes his head, bumping his elbow against my shoulder. "Didn't take you for insecure, Harp."

I blow out a sigh. "I like him," I admit, looking up at Leo. "More than I've liked a guy in a long, long time."

"You don't think he likes you? Spoiler alert: any guy who would willingly go to some girl's high-school reunion is interested."

"I don't know what to think. I mean, yeah, he likes me. Maybe he even cares about me. But the line between platonic and romantic is blurry as fuck. Every time we start to cross it, he backtracks and places us firmly in the friend zone. I don't want to get my hopes up for something that may not pan out. And I'm not willing to indefinitely settle for this in-between thing we've got going on. I've already let this go too far. You know me, Leo. I'm an all-or-nothing kind of girl."

Leo is quiet for a long minute. "Yeah, but this isn't the same as being a straight-A student or a slacker. This isn't like you showing up early for work and staying late before taking some personal time off. This is just the way it is with dating. You're pinning some hope or expectation on a future desire, never knowing how it will play out. I get what you're saying about the in-between but if you wanted a direct answer, then you need to have a serious conversation with him. And...you're not."

I release a sigh. "Because what if he wants nothing?"

Leo shrugs. "Then you know to walk away. Because for you, isn't less than all still settling?"

I nod slowly. "It feels scarier now than it used to."

"That's because you got burned."

I look up, meeting Leo's eyes. "I'm not hung up on Sean. At all."

"I know. You're hung up on the fallout of him and Anna

betraying you. They shook up your confidence and now, you're scared to trust a guy. Even a friend."

"I'm friends with you."

"Because I'm forcing you to talk on these early morning runs." He lifts a challenging eyebrow. "How many friends have you made this past year? And how many of them are female?"

I roll my lips together, knowing he's right. Since my move back to Tennessee, I've gone out of my way to actively avoid people, friendships and connections, from my old life. And slowly, the friendships I had in Chicago have changed. The girls I connected with in college are still my girls, but our lives are moving in different directions. Most of them are married, growing families, or still living the single life that includes dancing on bars on Saturday and nursing a hangover on Sunday. I'm...somewhere in the middle.

I'm a freaking friend-girl.

Sighing, I toss my hand into the air. "I think you're right, Leo," I admit slowly, elbowing the one friend from my past life who made it into the present. He's quiet and I look up again. "Aren't you gonna tell me 'I told you so'?"

He chuckles and tosses an arm around my shoulder. "What the hell kind of a friend would I be if I did that, Harp? Just, give Barnes a shot. He's got it in him to live up to the expectation, to grow into the hope. Maybe he's not ready yet. Or maybe..."

"Maybe?"

"Maybe this weekend is a turning point."

I lean into Leo's side as we approach my building. "If his parents can get past the nose ring." I twist the blue crystal stud in my nose.

Leo laughs loudly and I join in. We say goodbye at the

front entrance, and I enter the lobby. Before I make it to the elevator bank, I jump in surprise. "Sean?"

Sean Collins stands from the sofa inside the lobby and walks toward me. "Hey, Harper."

"What are you doing here? How do you know where I live?" I ask, a little creeped out by his sudden appearance.

A blush works over his cheeks. "Your mom told me. We ran into each other at the supermarket." He pushes his hands into his front pockets and dips his head. "I was in the area. Thought I'd stop by."

Of course she did. Mom's taking this need for closure a little too seriously since I'm over it. Ever since I've met Damien and saw Anna and Sean at the reunion, I've mentally let go of a lot of the hurt and anguish their betrayal caused.

Apparently, Sean did not. Because there's no way he was casually in the area, so far from his place of work, this early on a weekday morning.

"Um, okay. What's up?" I ask.

Sean shrugs, removing his hands from his pockets. "Want to grab a coffee or something?"

I blow out a sigh. "Sean, I'm—"

"Come on, Harper. You're not seriously dating an NHL player, are you? It's not going to last, babe. He's going to be on the road a lot. The demands of his career aren't for—"

"Don't finish that statement, Sean." I back up toward the elevators. "I was going to say I have to get to work. But, whatever you're selling, I'm not interested in buying. Been there, done that. Remember?" I jab at the call button.

When the elevator arrives, I step inside and ignore the crestfallen expression that ripples over Sean's face. But he's got to be kidding me. Does he think he's going to win me back—if that was even a possibility—by insulting my choices?

I take the elevator back to my apartment and push Sean from my mind. Entering my space, I look around.

It feels less lonely than it did at the start of the summer. It houses an energy that was lacking before Damien barreled into my life. Before I befriended Leo again. Before the guys on the Coyotes started inviting me to their summer happy hours at Corks. I've only gone to two and dipped out early after one drink, but maybe I should make more of an effort. Maybe next week, I'll accept one of their regular invitations and get dinner and drinks with a potential new friend group.

I may have moved back to Tennessee but I'm not the same woman I was when I left. I have regained some of the confidence I've lost. I've faced some of the fears that have plagued me for the last few years. I've moved on from my high-school drama and the baggage I've carried around since Anna and Sean hooked up. I've evolved.

I take a shower, blow-dry my hair, and get dressed for the day. Before I head to the office, I grab my sexiest piece of lingerie and drop it into the suitcase I pulled out last night.

Maybe Leo's right. Maybe this weekend is a turning point.

If it is, I want to be prepared.

————

THE CLOSER WE get to Connecticut, the tenser Damien becomes. At first, I wonder if he's a nervous flier. Then, with how frequently his eyes keep darting to my phone, I wonder if he saw one of Sean's texts that I keep deleting.

Sean: I'm sorry, Harper. Can we start over?

Sean: Harper, let me explain. Can I take you to lunch? Coffee?

Sean: My dad would really love to see you. Please come by the shop this week.

Delete. Delete. Delete.

Turns out, I don't think it's either of those things. By the time our plane lands, Damien's shoulders are nearly around his ears and his demeanor is the most aloof I've ever witnessed.

We emerge from the airport and Damien waves to a driver idling at the curb. "Samson."

"Mr. Barnes, good to see you, sir." Samson steps forward to take our luggage and place it in the trunk.

I freeze, my eyes darting from Samson, to Damien, to the sleek black limousine.

"You good?" Damien asks, softly touching my elbow.

"You seriously downplayed your upbringing."

Fear flares in his eyes as he clears his throat. "I told you. *Gossip Girl.*"

I nod, realizing he did. But for some reason, hearing it and seeing it are two very different things.

"Will you still come?" he asks.

At the worry in his tone, I soften, placing a hand on his hip. "Of course. Damien, I'm here. You and I are in this together, whatever this is."

Relief replaces the fear. "I thought if you knew the extent of it, you'd bail."

My eyebrows knit together in confusion. Damien's demeanor, nervous and unsure, is unlike him. It's unnerving to see a man who is always put together start to unravel at the seams. "You really thought I'd bail on you?"

"No." He shakes his head, backpedaling. "Not me—

this." He lifts a hand in the direction of the limo and a patiently waiting Samson.

"This is you if it's your family. Your history," I tell him. "The same way the reunion was mine. And you showed up for me."

Damien nods, a hesitant smile curling the corners of his mouth. "I'm happy you're here, Harper."

"So am I." I mean it too. Right now, there's no place I'd rather be than supporting my guy...whether he be a friend or something more. Please, I hope something more.

Damien clears his throat and stands straighter. The aloof, borderline indecision, that crept into his irises during our flight here evaporates. Instead, it's as if he's made a decision and is embracing it fully. His hand wraps around mine and he tugs me toward the car. Opening the door for me, he smirks. "After you."

I slide into the limo, introduce myself to Samson, and make small talk.

As we leave the airport and drive toward Damien's childhood home, the houses outside my window grow farther apart. Siding gives way to brick and stone. Driveways give way to private roads.

Silence descends in the limo as we drive up a long, private road that turns out to be the entrance to the Barnes's estate. We come to a stop in front of a massive mansion with a horseshoe driveway and multiple luxury cars parked out front. Damien releases a long exhale.

"Welcome to my family's home, Henderson."

I nod, pulling in a restorative inhale. "We got this, Barnes."

He chuckles, the sound surprising us both. "You know, I believe you."

"Good." I step out of the limo when Samson opens the door.

As I round the limo, thanking Samson as he pulls my rolling suitcase from the trunk, the ornate front doors open and members of Damien's family spill onto the front steps.

"I'm so happy you're here!" a woman in her sixties, I'm assuming his mother, squeals.

A tall man with the same bright green eyes as Damien wraps an arm around her shoulders.

"Uncle Damien!" a little boy, about four or five years old, hollers. He races to Damien's feet and throws his arms around Damien's legs.

"Christ, Garrett, have you grown," Damien says, lifting the boy and sitting him on his shoulders. "What's Mama been feeding you, huh? Lions?"

"Don't take the Lord's name in vain," a woman, who I think is Damien's sister, Fiona, admonishes.

Garrett giggles.

"Take it easy, Fi," a guy, I'm guessing Fiona's husband, Gary, says.

With his nephew on his shoulders, Damien turns and extends his arm in my direction. I step forward, smoothing my skirt down my legs so I don't fiddle with my nose ring. Damien takes my hand and together, we approach his family.

Their gazes roll over me, more curious than anything else. Fiona tilts her head, studying me. Damien's dad lifts his eyebrows. His mom leans closer.

"Everyone," Damien says, his demeanor bordering on formal. He squeezes my hand once. "Meet my girlfriend, Harper Henderson."

Girlfriend.

Not friend.

Not friend-girl.

But *girlfriend*.

He owned it. His voice was strong and steady. His grip on me never wavered.

I beam and give a little wave. "It's nice to meet you. Thank you for having me this weekend, Mr. and Mrs. Barnes. You have a beautiful home and I'm happy to celebrate such a wonderful occasion with you and your family."

Mrs. Henderson shifts closer and envelops me in a stiff hug. "It's good to meet you, Harper."

"Why didn't you tell me about her, mate?" his brother-in-law asks, wagging his eyebrows.

Fiona hushes him.

Mr. Henderson pulls me into a warm embrace, his eyes brimming with delight.

"Damn, you really brought her?" Another guy steps onto the porch. By his resemblance to Damien, I guess it's his brother, Charlie. He pulls Damien into a hug and whispers, "You're a brave man."

Damien shakes his head, smirking. "Nah, she's a fearless woman."

I like the sound of that too.

TEN
DAMIEN

WATCHING Harper charm my dad makes something tight inside my chest unravel. While a part of me knows I should walk over to the table where my dad peppers Harper with questions and she gesticulates wildly with her hands, her signature smile on display, I hold back.

Because Harper made my dad laugh three times in the last ten minutes. When was the last time I made his eyes crinkle at the corners? Or caused a loud, somewhat surprised guffaw to fall from his mouth?

I invited Harper home at my dad's insistence, but I never thought he'd enjoy her company this much. The realization fills me with pride; I'm damn proud of Harper.

"He likes her," Fiona says from behind me.

Turning, I nod at the wistful expression on my sister's face. She moves around the kitchen like she still lives here, and I wonder how much time she spends with Mom now that she doesn't go into the office. Does she miss it? Does she still think about quarterly reports and bottom lines?

I open my mouth to ask when Fiona mumbles, "Mom forgot to buy almond butter."

I slide onto a barstool and watch my sister make my nephew a cream cheese and jelly sandwich. We're having an early dinner with friends and family but there's no way Garrett can last that long. "How are you, Fi?"

My sister looks up, startled. "Huh? I'm fine."

I tip my chin down and really look at Fiona. There are a few more fine lines radiating from her eyes. The corners of her mouth are pinched. She looks...tired.

I hunch forward and lower my voice. "Seriously. How are you?"

At the sincerity in my tone, my sister sags. Her shoulders drop and her lips part. "I'm exhausted, Damien." She tries to smile but it falls flat. Fiona places her palms facedown on the kitchen island and heaves out a sigh. "I'm exhausted and unmotivated and bored. I love my son more than life itself. Gary and I are...well, we are what we are. But I want *more*. I miss working. I miss waking up in the morning and getting dressed up. I miss chatting with my secretary and exchanging silly email threads with some of the other women in finance." She rounds the kitchen island and sits down on the stool next to mine, Garrett's sandwich momentarily forgotten. Fiona reaches for my hand and her eyes dart to the table where Dad and Harper are deep in conversation. "She's bright."

"Harper?"

Fiona nods. "She's energetic and exciting. I get it. But this world, our world, would stamp out her light." A shadow passes through my sister's eyes. "She deserves better than this, Damien. If you're serious about her, don't capitulate to Mom and Dad's demands."

"Come on," I say, gently. "They're more like expectations than demands."

My sister offers me a sad smile. "Maybe for you, yeah. You made your dream career come true."

"Yeah," I agree. Playing in the NHL was always my dream and a few seasons ago, after years of playing in Europe, I finally signed with a team. Now, I'm starting left wing for the Thunderbolts and while we didn't play in the Finals this year, our season was better than anyone imagined.

We're better than most people believed. Next season will be a whole new level and I'm ready for it. I *want* it.

Fiona drops her hold on my hand. "Mom and Dad are going to press you for what's next. You know that, right? You can't play hockey forever, Damien. And now, with you bringing Harper home..."

"You think they want me to get married?" Alarm rises in my throat.

Fiona laughs and slides from the barstool. "They definitely want you to get married. And move back to Connecticut. And work for the family business." Her eyes flicker over to Harper before meeting mine. "If you love her, keep her in Tennessee. This world isn't big enough for a woman like her."

My eyebrows knit together. Fiona opens a jar of jelly and resumes making Garrett lunch. Harper's voice rings out behind me, my dad's fourth laugh not far behind.

I know what my family's expectations are; I've known them since I was a kid. It's part of the reason why I chased hockey as hard as I have. It's partly why I've moved around and made my career the center of my life. On some level, I've always wanted my parents to accept me and the life I've created. But Fiona is right; they're going to ask what's next. What comes after hockey? How does it align with their vision for me?

I shift in my chair to look over at Harper. She glances up and catches my eye, shooting me a playful wink.

When did Fiona become so perceptive? She's right again; this isn't a life for Harper. But it's not the life I want for myself either. Still, sitting in my family's kitchen and watching Harper and my dad interact, hearing the admiration in Fiona's voice when she speaks about Harper, fills me with pride. My girl may not be from our world, but she could own it if she wanted to.

My sister's sigh draws my attention. She shakes some goldfish onto Garrett's plate.

The only thing is, Harper isn't my girl. And it's delusional to think anyone could ever own this world. Eventually, it chews you up and spits you out until you're exhausted and just a little bit broken.

Fiona is proof of that.

———

"SHE'S SMART," Dad comments to me before lunch, rattling off one of the qualities he values most in a person. Looks never cut it with Dad, only brains, wit, and common sense.

Harper is still upstairs dressing. Of course, because my parents are very much aware of my reputation, Harper and I are sharing a room. It shouldn't feel so illicit, but a spark of excitement runs through me knowing that tonight, I'll sleep with my body pressed against hers. I'm not planning to take advantage of this arrangement but I'm sure as hell going to enjoy the experience of watching Harper's breath even out and her eyes flutter closed.

"Very," I agree. "And she loves her work."

"I can tell." Dad clasps me on the shoulder as we walk

down the hallway toward the formal dining room. Staff have been here for the past few hours, setting up the table, preparing various dishes, and arranging flowers.

Mom is well-known for "throwing together" impromptu dinners but no one realizes how well-thought-out and executed those "spontaneous" occurrences are. And we have the hardworking cleaners, cooks, and event coordinators to thank for that.

"It's not every day you meet someone with that much passion," Dad continues. "At the company, everyone is a nephew or friend of someone else. That raw hunger is missing."

I snort. "The nepotism is that blatant?"

Dad squeezes my shoulder and shakes his head. "I'm trying to change things."

"Dad, don't take this the wrong way, but you're the one who started things." We enter the dining room, and I don't miss the way Dad's eyes cut to Gary, Fiona's husband.

Internally, I groan. From Charlie, I've learned of the financial hiccups Gary's decision making has caused in the past few years. If we're being honest, Fiona is better suited for Gary's position than Gary but..."I see your point," I concede.

Dad chuckles, the sound humorless. "I could use your sense of humor, Damien."

My throat thickens as I work a swallow. This is what Fiona was referring to. My parents are going to try to convince me to move home. I release an exhale. This isn't Dad making an off-handed comment, it's deeper than that. But are we bonding over the fact that my girlfriend—my *date*—reminded him that some people truly love their careers and hustle to obtain them?

Before I can respond, Charlie enters the space and

holds his hands wide. His eyes are glassy, and I try to squash the disappointment I feel toward my big brother, my former role model, for getting high to have dinner with his family. I thought he would have moved past his broken engagement by now. But when Felicity cheated on him, she didn't just make him a laughingstock in our social circles, she obliterated his trust in himself. "Damien, I'm sorry I had to take a few calls. But I want to learn all about this gorgeous woman you've managed to wrangle into this weekend."

I shake my head, not in the mood for Harper to play into my brother's antics. Charlie means well but everything is optics for him. A big gesture, a big display, a big moment. Anything to take the attention off himself and the demons he's dueling. As much as I love my brother, I don't want him pushing unwanted attention on Harper. I don't want her to feel uncomfortable with so many eyes and nosy questions directed her way.

I glance at the table. It's set for fourteen and I breathe out a sigh. It's not an unbearably large number of people. Mom and Dad's party is tomorrow, and this evening's gathering is just a few close friends of my parents. It's manageable.

"Come on, mate. You gotta share something with us. You're curious, aren't you, Gary?" Charlie continues.

Before I can respond, Harper enters the space and my breath lodges in my throat.

Christ, she is gorgeous.

Wearing a simple, sage-colored silk dress and nude heels, Harper looks like she just walked off the cover of a magazine. *Vogue*. She straightened her hair, and it hangs down her back like a waterfall. Her eyes are bright, her lips painted in a soft pink, and a small gold pendant is nestled into the hollow of her collarbones. Is it a locket? Is it important?

I want to reach out to touch it, to ask her about it. I want to know everything about this woman and punch my brother for prying.

I let out a slow breath, trying to get my emotions under control. I'm all over the place. A surge of protectiveness, a flare of pride, a shot of desire. When Harper is around, I feel too many things at once and I don't know how to manage that.

"What do you want to know?" Harper lifts a questioning eyebrow.

Dad laughs. Again.

Harper's grin grows.

Charlie's eyes spark with amusement, blotting out some of the detached glassiness. He gestures for Harper to take a seat and moves to the bar to prepare some drinks. I slip into the chair beside my girl before Charlie, or Gary, can claim it.

"You doing okay?" I lower my voice.

She turns toward me and smiles. "Never better."

Under the table, I slide my hand onto her thigh. "Thank you for being here."

She covers my hand with hers. "Thank you for trusting me."

I nod, unable to reply because my ability to breathe has faltered. I do trust her. I trust her more than I've trusted another person in my life before.

The realization is both calming and panic-inducing.

What does this mean? What do I want?

How the hell will tonight unfold?

Before I can properly dissect the questions popping to life in my mind, my mother and Fiona enter the dining room. Harper stands and I follow suit, interlacing our hands. I pretend it's for her benefit but right now, I need her strength. I need her courage.

Because I think I'm falling for my friend-girl.

And it both scares and delights the hell out of me.

ELEVEN

HARPER

THE DINNER IS A FANCY AFFAIR. It's a far cry from the family gatherings and casual Sunday dinners I enjoyed growing up. Instead of a roast Mom started preparing at dawn, there's a team answering to a head chef. Instead of my grandmother's chipped china, there's an aesthetically balanced color palette that required three changes in glassware until Mrs. Barnes gave her final approval.

Soft rock does not play from a speaker in the corner of the room. Instead, classical music wafts through speakers hidden in the ceiling. It threads through the various conversations like whispered secrets, gentle and soothing.

If it wasn't for the glass of wine in my hand, I'd be having a mini panic attack. But I promised Damien I could handle this weekend, that I would show up for him. So, here I am, dressed in silk, spritzed in my finest perfume, and armed with my sharp wit, a smile, and booze.

"You had one hell of a season, son." A man named Wells gestures toward Damien conversationally. He takes a sip of his wine and I try to remember if he's Mr. Barnes's business partner or Mrs. Barnes's long-time interior designer.

Damien straightens beside me. "Thank you. I'm looking forward to next season."

I turn to Damien. "Training starts in two weeks, right?"

His grin turns genuine as his eyes hold mine. "Yep. A week after you."

I chuckle.

A woman about my age at the end of the table leans forward. A frown pinches her brows. "What are you training for?" she asks me, not unkindly. Still, there's an edge to her voice. She's Wells's eldest daughter, Cecilia.

"Oh, I work for the Knoxville Coyotes. Our preseason kicks off next week." I lift my wine glass and gesture toward the entire table. "This is my last weekend of freedom and I'm happy to be celebrating with y'all."

Cecilia's sister, Gabby, winces at my use of *y'all*. Damien's hand finds my thigh again. Gary gives Gabby a reprimanding look and she lowers her eyes. Fiona's gaze darts between Gary and Gabby. Charlie chuckles, rubbing his hands together and leaning forward as if things are about to get interesting.

"It'll be pretty busy then, won't it?" Gabby asks. "For the two of you to spend meaningful time together." Again, her gaze cuts to Gary who pointedly ignores her and gulps his wine.

"I'd imagine so," Cecilia quips, glancing at Damien. "Damien's skipped our last two ski trips to Aspen." She pouts and I try not to vomit in my mouth at her desperation.

At how she's making a play for him right here, at the table, where I am sitting with his fingers curling into the material of my silk dress.

"Oh." Mrs. Barnes waves a hand. "He's going to try to

make it this year. Right, Damien? Surely now that you've made the team, you can have more free time to visit your family. And closest friends." She smiles at Cecilia.

"Will you and Fiona be joining this year, Gary?" Gabby asks, her index finger slowly tracing the rim of her wine glass.

Gary chokes on his wine and Fiona flushes. The grip on her fork tightens until her knuckles turn white. Damien squeezes my thigh, his jaw ticking.

What the hell is going on?

"Ah, last year was fun," Wells tosses out, painfully oblivious to the tension brewing around the table. "Garrett had a great time, didn't he?"

Fiona nods, still staring at her plate.

"You missed out on that, Damien." Mrs. Barnes pats her hair. "I know men have to work, but you don't want to miss seeing your nephew grow up." Her gaze softens as she looks at Fiona. "That's why it's wonderful that Fiona stepped back from the business to look after Garrett."

"Agreed." Wells raises his glass, glancing at his own daughters. "Gabby is set on studying business administration but really, once she's married, will she have use for that degree?"

"Ah, but the degree will help her land the husband," Mrs. Barnes laughs.

Beside me, Damien is so rigid, I'm worried he's about to crack. Charlie's eyes ping-pong around the table, lit with amusement. But when he speaks, his tone is sarcastic. "Unless she cheats with her professor first." He winces as soon as the words land and remorse lines his expression. I feel a pang of sympathy for the eldest Barnes sibling.

Damien winces and shakes his head, but I read the concern in his eyes as he looks at Charlie. Mrs. Barnes shoots Charlie a reprimanding look, more irritated than worried, and he drops his gaze to his plate.

Wells coughs into his napkin, as if the sound will erase Charlie's comment.

At the end of the table, Mr. Barnes dips his head and I get the sense that while he doesn't endorse his wife's, or Wells's views, he's not going to publicly contradict them either. Even though Charlie's comment was unnecessary, it's obvious that it came from a place of deep pain.

I place my hand on top of Damien's, flatten his palm to my thigh, and sit back in my chair.

As I listen to his mother speak, my understanding grows. She's clueless about his career and the type of commitment and discipline it takes to succeed in professional sports. She's also unaware of the surreptitious glances between Gabby and Gary.

But Fiona isn't. Fiona seethes silently, her anger masked by her hurt and humiliation.

"Well," Damien shifts again, one hand scraping against his jawline. "We don't have to take shots at everyone's career aspirations. No one thought I'd ever play professional hockey and the Bolts had a great first season. We—"

"But you can't play hockey forever," Cecilia cuts him off.

Mrs. Barnes smiles gently. "She's right, dear. What are your plans for *after*?"

Ouch. I bite the corner of my mouth to stop myself from speaking out of turn.

"After?" Damien's brow knits.

Fiona places down her fork, her eyes darting between Damien and me.

"After hockey," Mr. Barnes takes up the cause. "There's

always room for you at the company, Damien. We'd love to have you."

Hurt flickers over Damien's expression but it's gone in a blink.

Charlie tips his head, his eyes pinned to his father's.

A handful of silent conversations, nuanced with history, pregnant with expectations, simultaneously unfold. While my family has had their share of disagreements, they've always been voiced aloud. They've always been solved through honest conversation. None of this prodding while smiling. No hidden agendas voiced through polite conversation. Whatever is happening here is outside my comfort zone.

But it doesn't matter. I'm here for Damien. I promised to have his back. Taking a fortifying sip of my wine, I lean closer to the table. "What's wrong with enjoying the moment you're in?" I ask everyone. All the guests turn to look at me, surprised that Damien's girlfriend, a newcomer, would speak up. Perhaps I'm breaking protocol. "Damien has worked hard, tirelessly, for his position with the Thunderbolts. If he wants to keep that position, he'll have to keep showing up, proving his commitment, and his hunger. He'll have to remain focused on the now." I glance at Damien. "The future will always be there but to live out your childhood dream, no one should wish that away."

Mrs. Barnes stares at me, her expression placid, save for a flicker of concern flaring in her irises before she blinks it away. Mr. Barnes nods slowly. "It's a good point, Harper. Still, Damien, you know we're always here."

"Of course," Damien mutters.

I grin, my eyes darting to Cecilia. "I'm sure there will be plenty of time for Aspen in the future."

Fiona chokes on a chuckle. Cecilia huffs. Gabby narrows her eyes at me.

Mr. Barnes covers his amusement behind his drink.

Underneath the table, Damien's hand flips, palm up. He weaves his fingers through mine and squeezes in a silent thank you. I keep my eyes trained on the table and my ears tuned into the conversation.

For the first time, I understand what Damien meant about his world. His family isn't unsupportive of his career, but they're not fully behind him either. The circles they spin in require a skill set I've yet to develop.

I may have the thick skin and the sharp retorts. But I don't have the calculated foresight. I don't know how to wrap words with hidden meanings in a frilly bow.

And truthfully, I don't want to.

Will Damien ever want this life for his future? Or is living in the present enough?

Could a simple woman like me be enough for a complicated man like him?

———

BY THE TIME we're eating dessert, the tension at the table has dissipated. The guests are playing musical chairs, or taking drinks around the bar in the corner or in the comfortable chairs in the neighboring den. It's nice to sit back and watch Damien interact with his siblings, exchange conversation with his dad, and toss an arm around his mother's shoulders.

Gary disappears under the guise of checking on Garrett, but I notice how Gabby slips from the room a few minutes later. Unfortunately, so does Fiona. And a glowering Damien. Still, no one says a word.

Every now and then, Cecilia presses her interest, sidling up to Damien's side, placing a hand on his chest, or batting her lashes. And every time it happens, I watch the detached, aloof expression shutter over his face like closing elevator doors. One moment, he's open and joking, eyes bright. The next, he's perfectly polite but disengaged, holding himself apart from the rest of the room.

It makes me sad to think that Damien's lived his whole life this way, only letting his guard down in small, incremental moments with those closest to him. I like that he's more open with me, but I'd be lying if I didn't admit that sometimes, he is hard to read. He does close himself off. He reaches for humor when he doesn't want to be vulnerable, his default mode is an affable remoteness that is as frustrating as it is confusing.

"Did you have the cake?" Damien's voice fills my ear.

I turn into him, my body hyperaware of his hand as it slides over my hip. "I thought the party was tomorrow?"

He gives me a playful look of mock horror. "This is the rehearsal dinner."

I snort out a laugh. "A rehearsal for the anniversary?"

"Us Barneses like to go big at every opportunity."

My eyes drop to his trousers, and I blush. "I know."

Damien's laugh bursts out, loud, unchecked, and genuine. It causes me to blush and laugh with him, my hands slipping up his arms and wrapping around his shoulders. His fingers lace together at the base of my spine, and he cradles me to him, swaying slightly. In my peripheral vision, I see some family members and friends look our way.

I bet Damien doesn't laugh like that often, at least not at formal dinners. But he doesn't give anyone else his attention. Instead, his eyes are focused on me, holding my gaze, speaking to my soul.

The bright green, mischievous and playful like a cat, is a soft moss. Deep, soulful, and serious. "I'm happy you're here, Harper."

I roll my lips together, dipping my head in agreement. "Me too."

"No." He shakes his head. His left hand palms the center of my back as his right moves up my side, until his thumb lifts my chin and his long fingers wrap around the side of my neck. "You don't understand how significant this is. I've never brought a woman home before."

"Not even friend-girls?" I ask, reaching for levity. Not because I don't want Damien's truths, but I'm nervous to hear them in a room filled with his friends and family who I'm certain are now staring at us with blatant curiosity.

"You're my first that truly matters," he whispers, dropping his mouth to the shell of my ear. "You're my first everything that counts. And I don't know what to do with that."

I pull back slightly, meeting his eyes. "What do you want to do?"

He holds my gaze for a beat so long, a blush creeps up from my chest and fans out into my cheeks. "So many things, sweet girl." Then, he leans forward and presses a chaste kiss to my forehead. "Too many things," he adds, his voice rough.

His voice, the intent in his eyes, are in direct odds with his actions as he steps back and gives me a long look, followed by a smile.

But I hear the promise in his words and a shiver shimmies down my spine. Tonight, Damien and I are taking things to the next level. We're crossing the line we've carefully treaded for weeks.

This weekend is the tipping point I hoped for. And I have the sexiest piece of lingerie to celebrate it.

TWELVE
DAMIEN

LACE. Her sinful curves, her delectable ass, those full, mouthwatering breasts, are barely covered in scraps of sexy, black lace.

My brain short-circuits. A rush of heat flares to life in my bloodstream, nearly burning me from the inside out. Harper Henderson is in my bed, my childhood bed where I fucking fantasized about women half as beautiful as her, waiting for me to make a move.

And I need to. Move. But my feet are glued to the floor. My eyes are drinking her in, committing every inch of her body, the radiance of her blue eyes, the teasing smirk on her lips, the goddamn confidence that calls to me like a siren, to memory. I want to imprint it on the backs of my eyelids so every time I blink, I see Harper, like this. I recall that I'm not a complete fuck-up because this woman, with all her independence and intelligence, wants me. Chose me. Trusts me. She accepts me in a way no one ever has before.

"You're too goddamn sexy," I tell her, crossing the room.

"Did you have a nice drink with your dad and brother?" she asks sweetly.

"I'm not thinking about that." I lose my pants and begin to unbutton my shirt.

"I got it." She sits up straighter and begins to undo the row of buttons.

It's intimate, watching her hands undress me. Noting the concentration in the line between her eyebrows, the steadiness of her hands.

As she focuses on the buttons, the ends of my fingers graze over her bare thigh, trace the line of her lace panties that hug her hip. "You're making my fantasy come true."

She smiles, her hands parting the material of my shirt and pushing it off my shoulders. I shrug out of it and toss it on the floor. Harper's eyes drop to my boxers once before meeting mine. "Doing it in your parents' house?" She bites her bottom lip. "That's more cliché than the science lab."

I snort.

"But I find it hard to believe you didn't check that box in high school."

I shake my head. "I wasn't nearly as confident in high school."

Harper chuckles. "I think the society girls always had a soft spot for you."

"True," I concede. "But I never took them to my bedroom."

Harper shifts and leans back against the ridiculous number of decorative pillows at the headboard. This is Mom's doing. After I moved out, she kept our rooms mostly the same but added some touches—like pillows and artwork —to make them more cohesive with the rest of the house. "Where'd you take them?"

I sigh. "This is what you want to talk about?"

Harper laughs. "I'm curious. Not threatened."

"Good." I like that she's confident. I like that she knows

that her worth, her value, far exceeds mine. "Pool house, the game room..." I shrug. "I had one relationship in my life and now, I realize it never meant more than the moment."

She tilts her head, studying me. "And this?"

"This means more than tonight, you know that."

She nods, a vulnerability swimming in the depths of her eyes.

"I like you, Harper. I like kissing you. I like spending time with you. I fucking love seeing you here, in my bed, in my parents' home. I want you so fucking badly, but never at the expense of losing you. I don't ever want us to not be us."

"What are we?" she whispers.

My heart gallops, thumps in my eardrums. I feel off-center, desperate to touch her and love on her, but scared as fuck that I won't be enough. That eventually, I'll fuck it up. Barneses are good for that.

"Better than anything I've ever been before," I admit.

Harper holds my gaze for a long, drawn-out moment. Then, she reaches for me, and I shift into her. Her legs wrap around my hips, her hands find the tops of my shoulders. I dip into the cradle between her thighs, lower my body onto hers, careful not to let her bear the brunt of my weight, and push her hair back from her face.

"Are you sure about this?" I want her to know that once we cross this line, things will change.

How can they not?

But will they change too much?

I banish the thought, push the insecurity from my head.

"Yes. I want you too, Damien." Harper's eyes are wide, filled with longing and desire. "I've wanted you for a long time."

"You have me," I murmur, my voice cracking with raw emotion. Does she understand the depth of that truth? She has me more than any woman ever has before. She owns the pieces of my personality I keep locked away, slivers of my heart I never share.

Harper tips her chin up and I drop my mouth to hers, kissing her with a sensuality that turns my body both hot and cold. Fire and ice.

Our kiss is deep, filled with meaning I've never experienced before. I take her mouth the same way I want to take her: fully, intentionally, thoroughly. As Harper arches into me, the lace of her bra grazes along my skin, the pebbled peaks of her nipples hardening.

"Jesus, you're gorgeous." I palm her breast, loving the weight of it in my hand.

Harper moans and I drag my mouth away from hers, trail it down her neck, place open-mouthed kisses along her chest. Ripping down the lace cup of her bra, I draw her breast into my mouth, sucking deep before turning my attention to her sensitive nipple.

One hand drops between her legs and I trace the pattern of the lace before dragging it to one side and testing the wetness of her arousal.

Holy fucking shit. "You're soaked for me, baby."

"Want you," she murmurs, her hips arching up into mine.

I'm rock hard, a steel fucking pipe. I want her to pull off my boxers and position my hard length in between her sweet thighs. But first, I want to worship this woman for giving me more, making me feel more, than I ever have in my life.

Sliding my body down hers, I grab the sides of her panties. "Lift," I demand.

Immediately, her hips rise. I shimmy the sexy lace down her legs and discard them on the floor. From my vantage point, I see her arousal, glistening, waiting for me to feast. I can't stop myself from licking my lips and Harper must love the visual because she moans, reaching for me.

"Not yet, Harper." My palms slide up her inner thighs until I hold her open. I keep my eyes glued to hers as I slowly lower my head. The pure, unfiltered desire in her irises has my cock twitching in my boxers. But I want this to be good for her; I want this to be the fucking best it's ever been for both of us.

I drag my tongue slowly up her center, chuckling as she bucks against me. Then, I set to work, tasting her, sucking on the bud of her clit, lapping as her sweetness rolls over my tongue.

"Damien," her voice is raw. Wanting.

I don't respond, just pick up my pace. Her thighs begin to shake, her fingers rake through my hair, tugging. I know she's close and the realization that I can make a woman as steady as Harper lose control pushes me into a frenzy. I eat her pussy like it's prime fucking rib. In fact, it's better. And she snaps, crying out as her body quakes with an orgasm. I let her ride it out against my face, loving that her hand reaches down to catch mine. Clasping my fingers tightly, she comes back to the moment.

When I pull back, brushing my thumb over my lips and sticking it in my mouth, her eyes nearly fall out of her head. "Damien."

"You're too fucking sweet for your own good, Harper."

"I, wow," she breathes out, glancing around her room. "I've never, that was—"

"For me too."

Confusion ripples through her eyes. "We haven't gotten to you yet."

"No," I agree. "But watching you, helping you reach a climax was the best thing I've ever witnessed in my life."

Harper chuckles, but her expression is uncertain, a little shy, a little embarrassed.

"I can't wait to do it again," I admit.

She smiles now, a full-on beam of radiance. "Really?"

"Really," I say, knowing that this moment matters. This moment is the verbal commitment beyond the physical act. It's the next step and I want to take it with Harper.

She motions for me to come closer. "Come here."

I fall over her, covering her body with mine. Her legs wrap around my waist again but this time, probably because I'm not expecting it, Harper rolls us until she's straddling the tops of my thighs. Her hot hands dip into the waistband of my boxers. "Lift," she demands.

I do so gladly.

The second she pulls off my boxers, my dick springs to life, desperate for her touch. But she surprises me again. Instead of reaching for me, she slips down my legs and bends over, drawing me into her mouth.

As her lips wrap around my cock, I see fucking stars. She grips the base of my dick, tugging slowly as her tongue swirls over the tip. It's sexy as hell and when she flips her hair over her shoulder and meets my gaze, it's the most erotic moment of my life. I swear I think she fucking winks and then, she sets a pace. She works her hand and mouth in perfect tandem that has me panting, reaching for her long, dark hair, clenching the bed sheets.

"Harper. Baby, slow down," I wheeze out.

She chuckles, straightening, her hand still working my shaft. Biting her lower lip, she turns her sexy sapphire eyes on mine. "Can I?" she asks, positioning me at her entrance.

"Fuck yes," I say, sitting up on my elbows so I can watch

it happen. I want to remember the moment my cock disappears inside of her forever.

She doesn't hurry though. Instead, she keeps sliding her hand up and down my length. "Condom?"

"Shit," I laugh out, closing my eyes. "I can't believe I almost fucking forgot."

Harper bites the corner of her mouth. "I'm on the pill, Damien. And I'm clean."

My eyes pop open. What the hell is she saying? Is she suggesting— "Harper, I, what?"

Nervousness floods her eyes and I backtrack.

"I'm clean too, Harper. But I—this is a big step. This is a lot of big steps." My eyes zero in on my dick in her hand. "Are you sure?"

She nods slowly.

"I need to hear the words," I say, needing to know that she's not going to regret this. If she regrets anything with me, it will shred me from the inside out. "Because I've never barebacked with a woman before."

"Yes," she whispers. "I trust you, Damien."

"Harper," I say, unsure of what to say next. *I care about you. I'm falling for you. I don't know how to manage all the things I feel when you're near. I'm going to fucking die if you don't sit on my dick.*

She shifts again, her knees pressing into the mattress by my hips. Then, she sinks down on me with a slowness that is so erotic, it should be triple X-rated.

"Fuck." I close my eyes and drop my head back, so many sensations moving through my body.

I'm so hard, so desperate for her, I can't think straight. At the same time, I want to make this good for her. I want to draw it out and remember this night for every night that comes after.

Harper begins to move, and I swear again. She rides me like her body was made for mine. I let her set the pace for several minutes before I take control.

Flipping her underneath me, I roll on top. I love the way her eyes widen with surprise.

"You're too fucking good at this," I say.

She laughs.

"Hang on, baby."

Amusement and want flare in her eyes. She grips my shoulders. Then, I move, thrusting into her with a pace that borderlines on frantic. We cling to each other, pouring dirty words and needy thoughts into each other's ears until she cries out again. She milks my cock as I pound into her, finding my own release.

"Harper, Harper," I chant her name as I come, falling over her body. I quickly roll onto my side, and pull her into me, holding her as our breathing settles and we both come down from the best natural high.

My cum drips down her thighs as I pull out and the visual of our mess causes my dick to jump, nearly ready for another round. "Jesus," I mutter, dragging a finger through it, smearing it over Harper's clit. She moans, still sensitive.

I look at her, find her eyes trained on mine. Licking my lips, I kiss her hard. "That was amazing."

She takes a deep breath that looks a lot like relief. Was she worried about my reaction?

I brush her hair back from her face. "Harper, I have a confession."

A flicker of panic flares in her irises and I hate that it's there at all.

"I know this started as a favor between neighbors."

Her nostrils flare and she nods.

"But I've caught feelings. Real ones. Harp, I'm fucking

falling for you." I slide closer to her, and grip her waist. I need to touch her. I need to hold her as I say words I never thought I'd say before. As I experience feelings I never thought I'd feel before.

I watch as understanding of what I'm saying dawns in her eyes. A small, surprised laugh falls from her lips before she smiles. "Really?"

"Really."

She kisses me. "Me too, Damien. I am too."

Her words fill me with a lightness; they make me feel like I'm floating. Being with Harper intimately, so damn beautifully, makes me feel invincible. Capable of being the man she needs me to be.

I pull back and drag the tip of my nose along her cheek. "Let me clean you up."

She laughs lightly. "What's that entail?"

A smirk curls my lips. I move off the bed and swing her into my arms, carrying her toward my bathroom. "I'll show you in the shower."

Harper laughs again and I wonder if it's always this easy with the right person.

Maybe I've put off relationships for so long because I never knew it could be like this.

That finding your person could make you feel like home.

THIRTEEN
HARPER

WHEN I WAKE the next morning, I'm smiling. It's cliche, corny, maybe even childish, but I can't stop the grin that splits my face. I slept...wonderfully. Soundly. Wrapped in cool sheets and the warm arms of Damien, I slept without the gnawing loneliness I'm used to.

Stretching out, I glance out the window to the blue sky and bright sunshine. I feel rejuvenated. I turn toward my bedmate and pause to drink in his sleeping form. Damien's expression is relaxed, his lips as sensual as always. In sleep, the humor he holds in the lines of his face and the sometimes detached distance that rings his irises are gone. Instead, he looks peaceful. Innocent and vulnerable and beautiful.

It makes my chest squeeze against my heart because I want to freeze this moment, remember him like this. Will this become my new normal? Will I spend my mornings waking up beside this man? Will his heavy palm anchor against my back in the middle of the night? Will our legs intertwine, and our bodies grow closer in sleep?

A thrill rolls through me. I hope so. Because last night

was one of the best nights of my life and I want more of them. More of this man and the way he makes me feel.

The insecurity that's wrapped around my limbs for years loosens. The doubt that rolls through my mind recedes. For the first time in years, I truly trust the man beside me. I believe his words; I feel safe with his actions. After last night, Damien Barnes and I are building a future. We have a tomorrow to look forward to.

Damien stirs, his eyes fluttering open. As soon as he sees me, he blinks and grins lazily. "Come here, beautiful." He tugs me closer and I go gladly, my mouth dropping to his in a good morning kiss.

"Mmm," Damien hums, gathering me against his chest and rolling onto his side. Our noses brush. "How did you sleep?"

"Like a baby."

"My baby."

His words shoot through me like lust. They shouldn't. In the past, I mocked boyfriends who called their girlfriends "baby" but now that I'm the girlfriend...oh God, am I Damien's girlfriend? I shiver at the thought. "Are we doing this, Damien?"

His eyes open and find mine. Hold. "Do you want to do this, Harper? Because I sure as hell want to. Want you."

I breathe a sigh of relief. "Yes," I say. "Me too."

Damien wraps an arm around my waist and pulls me even closer. I'm half lying on top of him and still, it feels too far. "Good." He kisses the side of my neck. "Because you're mine."

His.

It's another example of something I would have scoffed at in the past. I would have rolled my eyes and made a snide comment about being no one's possession. But I want to belong to Damien. I want him to possess every part of me and consume the rest.

I move my face until our lips are lined up. Then, I kiss him with all the want coursing through my veins. He stiffens immediately, dragging me on top of his body and holding me so close, so tight, it's hard to tell where I end and he begins.

Instead, we become one. Our kissing turns passionate, our hands desperate, our moans breathless. Damien lights my body on fire and I reciprocate. We detonate together, like fireworks, all color and light. All hope and heart.

———

MR. AND MRS. BARNES'S anniversary party is something out of a movie. The backyard of their impressive home is an endless estate. I didn't fully see it earlier but now, standing amidst the gardens, the stone walkways, the massive deck with a custom bar and firepit, my mouth drops open.

A tent has been set up for the party and inside, every-thing is decorated in cream and blush tones. Gold accents add a lavishness to the affair. Champagne flows freely, large floral arrangements give off a sweet scent, and all the guests are dressed impeccably.

In truth, this anniversary party reminds me of a wedding reception. It's elaborate and romantic, personal-ized and special. Mrs. Barnes looks stunning in a designer Elie Saab gown, and I brush my hands down the skirt of my dress self-consciously as I realize many of the other women present are bejeweled in diamonds, their dresses replete with feathers or pearls.

I'm wearing a simple, floor-length, cobalt blue dress

with nude heels. I could be going to dinner or a friend's birthday party. Even though Damien's eyes lit up when he saw me before the party, no one else at this event has spared me a second glance.

"Oh, there you are, dear," Mrs. Barnes says, linking her arm through mine.

"You look stunning, Mrs. Barnes. Happy anniversary."

"Thank you," she beams. "I'd love to introduce you to some of my friends."

"Thank you." I'm touched by her offer since I don't know anyone here besides Cecilia and Gabby, and I'm definitely not engaging them in conversation.

Fiona was recently pulled away by a nanny to attend to her son, and Charlie is nowhere in sight.

Damien was called into his father's office fifteen minutes ago and while he apologized profusely, it's not like I could beg him not to speak privately with his dad. Besides, I can handle my own at a party, even one as lavish as this.

"Of course," Mrs. Barnes says, pointing to a svelte blonde. "That's my cousin Grace. You'll love her; everyone does. Oh, and my stylist, Bethany. She's around here somewhere. You two should get acquainted as you'll be attending future galas with Damien."

My throat dries at the insinuation. Does she think I can't dress myself appropriately to attend a gala? Or does her referral to my future with Damien signify her blessing?

Something in her tone clues me in that she's not my biggest fan and yet her smile, her word choice, the way she clutches my arm all points to positive. To anyone looking at us, it would appear that Mrs. Barnes is taking a special interest in her son's date. *Girlfriend.*

But right now, I'm not so sure.

"Not to mention if you join us for the holidays this

year," she continues, giving me a wide smile. "We usually spend Thanksgiving in Aspen."

Internally, I groan, recalling the Aspen-centered conversation from last night.

"There you are." Damien appears next to his mother. He gives her a warm smile, followed by a hug, and she drops her hold on my arm to pat his back. "Happy anniversary, Mom."

"Thank you, love. I'm thrilled you joined us to celebrate." Mrs. Barnes pulls back. "Where's your father?"

"He's coming right now. Just had to—"

Mrs. Barnes holds up a hand. "Take a call. After thirty-five years, I know how it goes."

Damien smirks and looks at me. "You having fun?"

I open my mouth, but Mrs. Barnes beats me to it.

"We're having a lovely chat, Damien." Mrs. Barnes pats my back. "I was just telling Harper about skiing in Aspen for Thanksgiving. Make sure she meets Bethany and sets up a few stylist appointments."

Damien frowns, his eyebrows bending.

"What's that look?" His mom shakes her head. "You don't want her to be embarrassed when she accompanies you to the Founders Ball in October."

The Founders what?

Damien rolls his eyes.

Mrs. Barnes widens hers. "I'm just trying to prepare her."

Again, for *what*? But I don't voice the question aloud.

"Don't," Damien mutters, his voice low.

Mrs. Barnes shrugs. "Oh, I see your father." She moves in the other direction. "Make sure you try the mini crab cakes; they're divine." She waves at us before being pulled into several side conversations on her way to intercept Mr. Barnes.

Damien threads his fingers with mine. "I'm sorry."

"For what?" I ask, wondering what just happened.

I don't want to out Damien's mother and her rudeness to him, especially at his parents' party. Over the course of this weekend, I've witnessed every member of Damien's family, save for Gary, be physically present but mentally absent in several social situations. But their politeness always perseveres. With Mrs. Barnes, there's a cattiness that none of the other Barnes members give off.

"My mom..." he trails off, shaking his head. "She's desperate for me to be back in this world but I don't want her to scare you off."

"Never." I smile, even as my stomach tightens.

Damien chuckles. "You say that now, Henderson. You haven't seen all the ugly yet."

I shake my head but before I can inquire further, a tear-faced Fiona streaks pasts us, ducking behind a garden wall. Two seconds later, I spot Gary, hands clenched and a vein pulsing in his temple.

"Shit," Damien mutters, his eyes darting to his parents who luckily are wrapped up in a conversation. "Can you excuse me for a second?"

I frown, wondering what the hell is going on, even though I have some educated guesses. "Yeah, of course."

He darts off after his sister and brother-in-law. My stomach coils tighter into knots. Nothing awful has happened and yet, I feel strange. There's a sense of foreboding in the air. The events unfolding around me are off-putting, fore-shadowing something sinister I don't understand. Something I don't fully belong to but clearly, Damien does.

Sighing, I move toward the bar and order another flute of champagne. When a waiter passes, I snag two mini crab cakes. Mrs. Barnes was right: they are divine.

I people watch, studying the guests and the pleasant but not entirely warm way they interact with each other.

Sigh. Mrs. Barnes was also right; I'm not dressed appropriate for this kind of event.

A woman joins me at the bar. She's blonde and beautiful and... "Grace."

She smiles when her name pops out of my mouth. "You must be Harper." She holds out a hand. "My nephew's always had an impeccable eye."

I smile, shaking her hand. "It's nice to meet you."

"Likewise. I usually avoid these things, but I couldn't miss my cousin's party without hearing an earful about it." She mock grimaces and I chuckle. "Are you having fun yet?"

I pause, trying to formulate a polite response.

But Grace laughs and wraps an arm around my waist. Turning toward the bartender, she holds up two fingers. "We'll take two Aperol Spritzes, Jerry. Heavy on the alcohol, light on the spritz."

"You got it, Grace," comes the reply.

I lift an eyebrow and Grace winks.

"Only way to survive these things," she informs me. "Alcohol and hanging with a girl's girl."

I laugh lightly. "So, it's always like this?"

She clinks her glass against mine when Jerry sets them down and we both drink. "It's usually worse," she confides. "This is still pretty tame." Her eyes narrow as she takes in the mansion. "Charlie hasn't made an appearance yet, has he?"

"Not to my knowledge," I say, wondering what that means.

Grace sighs and turns thoughtful eyes on me. "He's been having a really rough time since his fiancée cheated on him."

"With her professor?" I guess, recalling his comment from the night before.

Grace nods. "She was in grad school. No one supported the move, all thought she should walk down the aisle and pop out a bunch of babies. Pregnant but not totally barefoot in the kitchen, overseeing the chefs, not actually cooking, is how the Barneses like their women."

I roll my lips together to suppress my laughter. While Grace is divulging nuggets of truth, she's careful to relay the information with humor.

"But," she continues, "Charlie supported her. He wanted a partner, a true marriage. He loved Felicity fiercely, put her on a pedestal." Grace dips her head toward mine. "That's a dangerous thing."

"Yes," I agree, thinking of Sean. Of how I used to view Sean, as the center of my world. My future.

"You really care for Damien, don't you?"

"Yes," I say on a breath.

"Even if he didn't play hockey."

I smile. "I had no idea he was an athlete. I'm more of a football girl."

Grace laughs. "Good. He needs a woman who is going to ground him. Who is going to have a life independent of his. Who is going to have his back with this lot." Her eyes scan the party. She looks at me again. "Deep down, the Barneses have big hearts. They're just buried too deep." A faraway look fills her eyes, as if she's lost in the past. "But if anyone can bring them closer to the surface, it's Damien."

Her eyes soften. "Damien and the right partner." She takes another sip of her drink.

"Thank you, Grace," I say, partly for speaking so highly of me and partly for shedding light on Damien's family.

"I hope you're that partner, Harper."

Again, Mrs. Barnes was right; I already love Grace.

FOURTEEN
DAMIEN

I FUCKING HATE this stupid hedge maze Dad had constructed for Mom on their twenty-eighth wedding anniversary. It's pretentious and unnecessary. Not to mention, a fucking maze.

Every time I think I'm gaining ground on Gary and Fiona, I take a wrong turn. Now, I don't know how to get the hell out of here either. It's been years since I've walked through this, scoffing at how ridiculous the whole thing is. But Mom loves it, loves English gardens in general, and Dad is an exceptional gift giver.

I stop, throwing my hands in the air in frustration. This is why I rarely come home. And why I certainly don't bring dates. But Harper isn't a date; she's my girl.

I may have been hesitant to bring her home this weekend but if we're going to do this, be together and build a future, then she needs to know what she's getting into. She needs to meet my family and they need to know the woman who's turning my life upside down. Even if I couldn't fully admit it until last night.

But of course, nothing goes according to plan where my family is concerned.

Charlie, the golden Barnes, is high on cocaine and banging a broken socialite in the maid's bathroom. Dad demanded that I get him under control before my mother discovers his shit. And guess what his explanation for going off the rails is? That his ex fucked him up. That supporting her the way he did with our community just for her to go behind his back and cheat messed him up so badly, the only way he knows how to cope is with drugs and women.

Charlie was too far gone to even look contrite when I interrupted his meaningless fuck. He scoffed and politely told the woman to get lost.

I blow out a sigh, my blood boiling, but my concerns for my siblings, for Harper, also heightening as I take another wrong turn.

Mom's forcing her opinions on Harper, already trying to scare her off with stylists and gala commitments. I know my mother wants me with a society girl. It's a fact she made known my junior year of high school when my homecoming date Brittney was a girl of "questionable family stock," but I didn't think she'd be pushy about it this weekend. Especially knowing I never bring women around. Wouldn't that have clued her in that Harper is special?

And now, now I'm lost in a fucking hedge maze, dealing with my crying sister and her subpar husband.

"Don't touch me, Gary!" Fiona's voice rings out.

Immediately, my hackles rise, anger rolling through my body. As if the sense of urgency spurs me forward, I finally find my way around the maze and venture closer to Fiona.

"It didn't mean anything, Fi," Gary's tone is pleading. "It was one night; a fucking mistake."

"If it was a mistake, you wouldn't have done it again,"

my sister sobs. "It wasn't one night, you fucking liar. It wasn't one night."

The heartache in Fiona's voice physically hurts to hear. Fucking Gary and his inability to keep it in his pants. I knew from the first time I met him that he wasn't good enough for my sister.

But he came from solid family stock and has a last name that means something. Even though his family lost a great deal of their wealth in the dot com crash of the early 2000s, their last name still holds clout. Even though my father had to give Gary a job, society still thinks he's smart enough to handle it. The whole charade is sickening and if I wasn't sure of my sister's love for him at the time of their marriage, I would've raised some concerns.

But I didn't because Fiona truly loved him.

Enough to step back from her career to be the wife he expected.

Enough to step back from her social life to be the mother he demanded.

Enough to lose too many pieces of herself only to be cast aside for some random fuck.

"Are you going to tell your father?" Gary asks after a lull and the fact that he asked that at all—that my father's reaction is more of a concern to him than Fiona's infuriates me.

Fiona laughs but the sound is borderline hysterical. "She's nineteen years old, Gary. Gabby's a fucking baby! She's getting ready for college."

Shit. Disgust sits heavy in the pit of my stomach. Gabby? I blanche. Even though I had my suspicions of their attraction, especially after their conduct at dinner last night, having them confirmed is revolting. I desperately hoped Gary hadn't crossed that line and the fact that he did sickens me.

"She's legal," is Gary's defense.

Before my sister responds, I stumble through the goddamn maze. "You fucking asshole." I barrel toward Gary, hyped up on anger and resentment, fueled by my sister's pain.

"Damien, it wasn't—" Gary's hands are in the air but I'm unstoppable. Before he can finish his words, my fist connects with his jaw, sending him back into a hedge.

His large, round body stumbles into the prickly green shrub before he bounces forward, dropping to his knees. "Fuck," he sneers, rubbing a hand over his face. His fingers come away bloody and I'm not sure if I'm relieved or annoyed that I busted his nose. I mean, surely, cheating on Fiona deserves more than a broken nose? And with the nineteen-year-old daughter of a family friend, no less.

I shake out my hand as a reflex but once the lack of a sting registers, I drop it to my side. I'm too angry, too buzzed on adrenaline to feel much anyway. "You okay?" I ask my sister.

Her eyes well with tears and they track down her cheeks softly. "I'm sorry you witnessed that," she murmurs, putting up the wall that all us Barneses have mastered.

Don't let anyone see your ugly. Don't let anyone get too close.

Maybe that's why so much of our world is ruthless and even though one may witness it, one never truly knows how it feels until it's happening to you. The lack of empathy is sickening.

"Fiona, come on, it's me," I say, slapping my palm against my chest.

"Fi, he fucking hit me," Gary warbles, climbing up.

I hold out a hand. "Come near my sister again and

hitting you will be the least of your problems," I say, my voice even. In control. As expected.

"It was one fucking night," Gary mutters.

"Fuck off, Gary," I bite out.

Fiona turns away, swiping at her tears.

Gary turns around, muttering to himself about feminism and fucking hedge mazes.

"You okay?" I ask Fiona again.

My sister takes in a cleansing breath, releasing it slowly. She straightens her spine and nods. "It wasn't the first time. I knew about the others."

My heart sinks but I keep my mouth shut.

"I just chose to ignore it because...well, what am I going to do? We have a baby—"

"Garrett is nearly five," I say softly.

Fiona's eyes flash. "He's young, Damien. And anyway, the pressure it would put on Mom—"

"Her social standing can take it. Half of her friends are on their third, or even fourth, marriages."

"Not to mention Dad's business." Fiona ignores me.

"He'd probably be relieved to get rid of Gary," I admit.

Fiona snorts but then shakes her head. "Gabby's so young. What the hell was he thinking?"

"He was only thinking with his dick," I mutter.

Fiona laughs, even as her tears fall. "I'm so humiliated."

"Don't be. He's the one who should feel humiliated."

Fiona wipes at her tears, taking deep, cleansing breaths. I rub her back and pull her into a side hug as she collects herself. "What do you want to do?" I ask softly. "I'll play this however you want."

My sister shakes her head, offers me a smile through watery eyes. "We better get back out there. Mom will know something's amiss and...if she hasn't caught Charlie yet, she'll certainly catch me crying."

I wrap an arm around Fiona's shoulders. "You should be happy, Fi. Your happiness is much more important than any of this." I gesture to the edge of the maze and party beyond it.

Fiona gives me a shaky smile. "If you love her, Damien, let her go." Her response startles me and I stop. "I'm not saying it to be cruel," my sister continues. "I'm saying it because I've never seen you like this with a woman before. And Harper, she's a good woman."

"Yeah, and I'm a good man. Not a cheater, Fiona. I've never been anything but honest."

"To a fault," my sister agrees. "But this world, *our* world, is weighed more favorably for men. Even more so than the real world. Here, the expectations on women are suffocating. Here, the demands on women are soul-sucking." Fiona sighs again. "Maybe it's just where my head is at today, or maybe I'm wrong and it's like this all over, at every economic level but...Harper deserves more than what Mom, this family, and our world can offer." My sister wraps her arm around my waist and squeezes. "And so do you, Damien. But you're a part of our world no matter how many miles you try to put between you and it."

I roll my lips together, too hurt to respond. I would never put Harper in the position Gary has put Fiona. I would never behave the way I've seen men—on rare occasions, even my own father—behave. I don't expect Harper to be barefoot and pregnant in the kitchen any more than I expect her to run a household with a full staff. All I want is her happiness.

The realization pulls me up short again because...could she be happy with me? Fiona is right about one thing: this is my world no matter how much I try to disregard it. My family is my family, my name is my name, and the world I get sucked into each time I visit home is ugly, petty, and fake, hidden under a veneer of sparkle.

"Come on," Fiona says, tugging me forward.

Pushing the thoughts—sinister and hurtful as they are—from my mind, I desperately want to find Harper. "You know how to get out of here?"

Fiona laughs. "Not as quickly as I'd like to."

As Fiona and I find our way out of the hedge maze, I ask, "Are you going to tell Dad?"

She gives me a sad smile. "What do you think?"

Her response is tough to hear because it's not the best way forward for her. Instead, Fiona will continue to wallow in her own heartache. Dad won't intervene to help, and Mom won't ease her burden because they won't *know*.

But deep down, everyone with eyes knows Fiona is too damn good for Gary.

Except he has a family and a name and is part of our world.

See? It's not all sparkle.

———

I'M relieved when I find Harper at the bar with my mom's cousin Grace. Out of everyone present, she's one of my top three favorite relations. She holds the title of Aunt even though she's not truly my aunt. I just wish she was.

"There he is! My favorite nephew!" Grace reaches for me and pulls me into a warm hug.

"I'm so glad you came, Aunt Grace."

She laughs. "At least someone is."

"Aw, come on now. Mom's happy you're here."

Grace laughs again. She and Mom have a tenuous relationship. They grew up as close as sisters but somewhere along the line, their paths diverged. Mom fell in love with my father, a self-made man who was enough of a prodigy and had a big enough bank account to win the approval of her family. Grace fell in love with an ex-convict who could have cured cancer and still wouldn't gain the stamp of approval. However, Grace married him anyway.

For eight years, she had strained relations with her family, but she lived in wedded bliss until her husband's untimely demise. Upon his passing, she began to build fences with the family that cut her off but always on her own terms. And, to everyone's disbelief and frustration, her husband left one hell of a life insurance policy that allows Grace to continue to live life on her own terms.

It's the best upset that's ever occurred in the Barnes family and makes me wish I remember Grace's husband from the one or two times I met him.

"I'll take whatever they're drinking," I tell the bartender who makes me an Aperol Spritz. I shift toward Harper and wrap a protective arm around her waist. "How are you holding up?"

"I'm fine," she says, smiling. But her eyes are dimmer than they were when she woke up in my bed this morning. Her shoulders are tighter when they press into my chest and her demeanor has shifted.

I want to ask her what's wrong, but I already know.

She met the Barnes family; she's starting to witness the ugly.

FIFTEEN
HARPER

CHARLIE'S ARM lands heavily around my shoulders. "So glad to meet you. Really."

I smile at him, noting immediately that he's high as hell by how blown his pupils are.

Next to me, Damien's body locks down and he grimaces. Ever since he ran off to follow Fiona, his armor is back in place. His eyes hold a faraway look, a blankness filtering over his expression even as he smiles, or nods, or engages in conversation.

I don't like it one bit, but I won't call him out here, in front of his family. Certainly not when he's balancing so much, trying to ensure his parents' party is a success. For someone who labeled himself as the black sheep of the family, I find it hard to believe.

As much as I like the Barneses, their world is tough to navigate. Not to mention, with all the hidden vices and shames, private betrayals and twinges of embarrassment occurring this weekend, it's bizarre that Damien choosing his dream career is somehow a stain on the family name. If playing hockey is an embarrassment, then I can understand why Damien has kept his distance all these years.

And yet, he brought me home...

He wants to build a future with me. He wants us to have a life despite all this spectacle and backstabbing. He wants *me*. I remember that as Charlie squeezes me a fraction too tight, as Fiona avoids my eyes, as Mrs. Barnes schedules me an appointment with Bethany.

When the party ends and the cleanup crew is hard at work, Damien and I change out of our party clothes and gather our luggage. We say our goodbyes and the only two people I embrace warmly are Grace, the other black sheep, and Mr. Barnes, who could adapt to any world and hold his own.

Grace holds me close for an extra beat. "You're good for him, Harper." She says it like a reminder, like something I'll need to hold on to as I become more invested in the Barnes family.

While Grace means the words as an encouragement, they land in my stomach like a warning. A sense of foreboding washes over me that I try to shake off by turning to Mr. Barnes.

"I look forward to hearing big things for the Coyotes this season." Mr. Barnes smiles. "And the next time Jeane and I are in Knoxville, we'll do dinner at your favorite restaurant."

I grin back. "Thanks, Mr. Barnes. I look forward to introducing y'all to the Rib Shack."

Mrs. Barnes pales but Mr. Barnes laughs heartedly, wagging a finger at me. "I'm holding you to that, Harper."

Damien shadows my back, nudging me closer to the limousine. He hugs his dad and brother goodbye, exchanges kisses with his sister, mom, and Grace. Then, he slips in beside me and waves once as Samson drives us back to the airport.

We're silent for most of the ride save for an exchange of small talk with Samson. Damien holds my hand, his grip tight on mine, as if he's worried I'll slip away.

I assume he'll relax the closer we get to the airport, the closer to home, but tension continues to roll off him. It isn't until we enter his penthouse in Knoxville that he blows out a big sigh.

"Are you okay?" I ask gently.

He nods, lacing his fingers behind his head and walking to the floor-to-ceiling windows that overlook downtown. "I'm sorry."

I frown. "For what?"

His eyes flash as they meet mine. His hard exterior—all polite smiles and standoffish glances—melts away. For the first time, I see his anger, his hurt, his pain and I reach for him. Before I can wrap my arms around his waist, he grips my arms and stops me. "For today. It was...fuck."

"It was what?"

"My family wasn't fair to you, Harper."

"They weren't that bad."

He snorts and shakes his head. "My mom is ready to turn you into her protege. Because *that* worked out so fucking well for Fiona."

"Is Fiona okay?"

Damien mutters a swear. "Gary's stepping out on her," he admits, some of his anger subsiding as he deflates, agony blazing in his expression. He drops my arms and moves farther into the living room.

"With Gabby?"

He nods, swearing. "She deserves so much fucking more than what she got. And I wonder..."

"What?"

He turns toward me, his eyes cutting. "I wonder if she would have chosen different, better, if she felt supported. But my mother wanted her with Gary, or a man like Gary—"

"Wealthy?" I guess, trying to keep up.

Damien scoffs. "A man with 'good stock.'" He air quotes, sarcasm heavy in his tone. "Whatever the fuck that means." Damien drops to the couch, and I take the seat beside him, angling my body toward his.

"My mother always gets what she wants," he mutters ominously.

I nod, brushing my fingers through his hair. "What do you want?"

His eyes flicker to mine, unreadable. "This. With you."

"You have me."

A sad smile glints off his mouth. "But can I keep you?"

I furrow my brow, silently asking what he means. But my guy is hurting so when he tugs me closer instead of answering, I go willingly.

He kisses me soulfully, with emotions he doesn't know how to show, words he can't say. His hands come up to hold my cheeks and he frames my face, pulling back to look deeply into my eyes. "No matter what happens, this is real."

I hang onto his wrists, nodding. "We'll figure everything out, Damien. I know this weekend was tough but I'm here."

"Yeah," he says, not fully convinced. "I know."

I frown, wanting him to trust this. To trust me.

Instead, he kisses me again. Harder this time, with want and desire eating up his concerns. We make love on his couch, with the lights on, the curtains open, and the city shining around us.

It's passionate and intense. Needy and desperate. It's light and dark and brimming with love.

When we're finished, we lie in silence, staring up at the ceiling. Damien draws lazy figure eights on my upper arm. He's lost in his own thoughts, and I don't want to interrupt because I'm still trying to process how the hell I orgasmed three times in one night.

My phone beeps and I sigh, not wanting to deal with the real world when I can stay wrapped up in Damien and our bubble.

I reach out and feel my way over the coffee table until I grasp my phone. When I read the message, I frown.

Sean Collins: Hey. I just want to grab a bite and talk. That's it. Come on, Harp, hear me out.

"What the fuck does he want?" Damien growls.

I jump, momentarily forgetting that a message from Sean—something so inconsequential to me—would frustrate him.

I drop the phone back onto the table and turn into Damien's side, my bare breasts pushing into his rib cage. "Apparently, he wants to apologize."

Damien's muscles lock down as he nods tersely. "He been messaging you a lot?"

"I just ignore him. Ever since he showed up here—"

He shifts to look at me fully, his arm slipping from behind my head, and my head thumps against the couch cushions. Damien hovers over me, his expression tight, carefully neutral. "He came here, to your apartment?"

"Damien, it doesn't mean anything. Sean—"

"Of course it does." He cuts me off. "Sean wants you back."

"Sean wants me to forgive him."

"And do you?" he bites out, his lips pressed into a line.

"I'm over it. Yeah, I forgive him. And Anna."

"Since the reunion?"

"Since you," I admit. "Since the reunion and building a life here and meeting you."

"Then why is he still trying to take you to dinner?"

I snort and shake my head. "It's not like that."

"Maybe not yet," Damien's tone holds a note of forewarning, and he flops back next to me on the couch. "But it will be," he says quietly, sadness filling his voice. "We're both going to get crazy busy. Two people who haven't been in a real relationship in years..." he sighs. "Two people who are career focused, driven and ambitious, trying to balance it all..." He turns toward me again and drags my body on top of his. "I want to keep you, Harper."

"Damien," I breathe out, the dire picture he's painting scares me. It's unsettling because there's truth behind his words. We've been building our relationship in the easy months of summer, when both our teams are off, when demands on our time are limited. I've been working half from home and half from the office. We've been getting lunches and having impromptu coffee dates. "We're going to figure everything out."

His hands tangle in my hair, and he lifts his face to kiss the tip of my nose. "I fucking hope so, baby." He lowers his head to the couch again and stares at me. "I really do."

Then, he shifts us until we're sitting on the couch. Scooping me into his arms, he walks toward the bathroom. "Let's shower this mood off and go get some ice cream."

"Ice cream?" I try to search his eyes to understand the sudden shift in his mindset.

He nods, setting me on my feet. "Sure, one last hurrah."

"Damien—"

He flips on the shower faucet and smirks at me. "Tomorrow, you go back to work full-time and I start kicking up my workouts."

"Back to the real world."

"Yeah," he says, stepping into the shower.

The steam wraps around him and I take a moment to admire the planes of his body, the hard ripples of muscle, the way water drips off his skin. He manages a smile and beckons for me to join him. I shake my head, but he reaches out and tugs me under the stream of water.

Laughing, I wrap my arms around him. "I wish we could stay like this, Damien. Wrapped up in our own world."

"It's a hell of a lot better than the real world," he muses, before kissing me hard.

We have sex again in the shower before toweling off. Dressed in shorts and tanks, with wet hair, we clasp hands and walk a few streets over to an old-timey ice cream parlor.

It's a sweet way to cap off our summer break. But there's a nostalgia in it too; it's like our first real date occurred when everything else is falling apart.

I can't pinpoint exactly what's shifted but the lightness of Saturday evening is gone. In its place is a sense of dread, simmering just under the surface, that I don't want to give into.

As I dip into my mint chocolate chip ice cream cone, I try to push away the negative thoughts. After all, I'm embracing a new beginning. And Damien Barnes is still by my side.

SIXTEEN

DAMIEN

MONDAY
8:06 AM

Me: Hey, want to grab a coffee? Breakfast?

Harper: Already at the office! Dinner tonight?

Me: Going to Devon's for a team dinner. Everyone is back in town. See you after?

Harper: Absolutely! XO

12:04 **PM**

Me: How's your day going?

Harper: Crazy busy. Heading into a meeting. See you tonight?

Me: Good luck!

7:18 **PM**

Harper: Honey, I'm home!

Me: Just got to Devon's. Call you on my ride back?

Harper: Yes, please! (Kiss Face Emoji)

10:43 PM **Missed Call**

11:04 PM **Missed Call**

11:07 **PM**

Me: You must be sleeping. Sweet dreams, Harp.

TUESDAY
6:51 AM
Harper: Good morning!

7:19 **AM**

Me: Morning, beautiful! How's your morning?

Harper: Early run with Leo. On my way into work.

Me: ???

Harper: Car wouldn't start. I'm in an Uber.

Me: Why didn't you call? I would have given you a ride.

Harper: Didn't want to wake you.

Me: Always wake me.

Harper: (Heart Emoji) I'll remember that. Dinner tonight?

Me: Yes. Tacos?

Harper: Please! See you around 8 PM.

Me: Can't wait.

.   .   .

6:04 **PM**

Harper: Damien! I'm so sorry but I have a meeting that just appeared on my calendar. I won't be home until after 9 PM.

Me: I'll bring you dinner...TACO TUESDAY!

Harper: It pains me to miss out on taco Tuesday but it's a business dinner. I'm sorry; I'll make it up to you.

Me: Don't worry. I'll see you after.

Harper: I'll call you when I get home.

10:33 PM **Missed Call**

10:34 **PM**

Harper: You awake?

10:42 **PM**

Harper: You must have passed out. Hope you sleep well. XOXO

WEDNESDAY

Me: Hi, baby. I've got a team bonding thing today in the middle of nowhere.

Harper: ???

Me: It's some camping, hiking shit that Devon put together last minute. I won't be back until tomorrow.

Harper: Doesn't he know glamping is more your style?

Me: (Wink Face Emoji) Clearly, no one knows me as well as you.

Harper: (Laughing Face Emoji) Have a good time. I'll miss you.

Me: Miss you too. See you tomorrow?

Harper: Yes. No matter what. XX

————

"BREATHE IN THAT MOUNTAIN AIR," Cole announces as he hikes like a damn professional.

"You're way too chipper about this," River Patton, another one of my teammates, mutters.

"He got laid last night," Devon says.

"Hey!" Beau hollers. "That's my sister."

Cole's ears turn red, and I laugh.

The team is trekking through some woods in the middle of nowhere, all in the name of team bonding.

"I think I liked last year's field day better," I mutter, to no one and everyone.

"Same," Axel agrees, jumping on a rock. "Although there is something nice about being in nature."

I wrinkle my nose, unconvinced. All I've got to show for today is a fuck-ton of mosquito bites and a sweat-soaked T-shirt. This is not my scene.

And we have to pitch a fucking tent and sleep here like a bunch of Boy Scouts.

"You hate this," Patton comments.

I chuckle but he's not far from the truth.

Patton keeps pace with me. "How was summer?"

"Good."

"The women?"

"Only one," I admit.

"Seriously?"

"The right one," I amend.

"Shut the fuck up. You locked down a wifey?" Patton's clearly surprised because out of all the guys on the team, he and I are the only starters who are still single.

Well, I guess technically Beau Turner is too, but, to my knowledge, he doesn't hook up with random women. At least, he doesn't flaunt it. I've heard he's still hung up on an ex, his high-school sweetheart who made it big out in LA, but he doesn't like to talk about it much. In fact, out of all the guys, Turner keeps the most to himself, sharing even less than I do.

"Who is she?" Patton presses.

"Her name is Harper Henderson and we're together. Harper is...well, she's too fucking good for me."

Patton snorts. "Aren't they all?"

"What about you?" I turn the tables. "How was summer?"

Patton chews the corner of his mouth, a flare of unease shooting through his eyes.

I raise an eyebrow, waiting. We trudge up the stupid hill.

"Almost there," Devon calls out.

"I never took him for a nature-loving guy," I mutter.

Patton shrugs, looking away. "Same. And summer was summer," he says finally. "Now, I'm ready for the season."

"Yeah," I agree, reading the words he doesn't voice.

What happened during Patton's summer isn't something he's bringing along for the season. However he feels about that is his business and he wants me to let it go. So, I do.

Because I'm already worried that my summer love isn't going to last the season either. It's only been a few days and I am desperately missing my girl. Can we make this work? The hectic schedules, the travel, the unknown?

Can it be enough when Harper is Harper and I'm just me?

———

THE RAIN STARTS as a slow drizzle. I glance up into the darkening sky and pray that one of my teammates calls this, now, before the skies open up and we're all drenched by the rain. My sneakers already feel soggy from the damp ground, and I dread the thought of wading through puddles.

"We could set up camp over here." Cole points to a clearing before glancing up at the thunderclouds. "Don't want to get caught in the storm."

Couldn't he have suggested going to Corks for beers instead? That sounds like a much better way to bond than to pitch a tent in the middle of nowhere. Shit, do I have cell reception?

I move to pull out my phone when Devon points at me. "Barnes, Turner, want to start clearing away those branches?"

Ugh. I bite back my honest response to that question and turn to follow Turner.

Beau and I begin to move a bunch of branches as the other guys start to set up the tent. I guess, all things considered, my job is better since I don't know the first thing about putting up a tent.

"How's it going?" Beau asks.

I shrug. "Same old. You?"

He's quiet, thoughtful. "Okay, I guess."

"You seeing anyone?"

He narrows his eyes at me. "No one in particular. How're things with Harper?"

I toss a branch. "Let me ask you something."

Beau straightens, turns, and gives me his full attention.

"You think relationships, real ones, can work when the whole future is a question mark?"

Beau swears and grips the back of his neck. "Sure, I think they can." He tips his head toward Cole. "Look at the Rookie and my sister. Or Devon and Mila."

"That's new though." Both of those couples have been together a year or less.

Beau sighs and tosses another branch. "I don't know, man. I'd like to think so but the one time I tried…"

"Didn't work out?"

His expression is gutted, his eyes bleeding a pain he rarely shows, when they snap to mine. "Didn't work out," he confirms, but it's more than that. His relationship not working out leveled him.

And I know, deep down, that Harper could level me too.

I open my mouth to ask what happened, but a gale of wind kicks up and the rain beats down, hard and relentless.

"Get in the tent!" Axel hollers.

Damn, how'd they get that up so quickly? Cole is tossing our backpacks inside the shelter as River pulls in a small cooler.

The six of us huddle into the fairly large tent, sitting on the cold ground. Devon reaches into a cooler and passes us all a beer. We crack them open and lift them up.

"To the Bolts," Devon says.

"The Bolts," we all repeat.

The conversation turns to the upcoming season, our fiercest competition, and hockey in general. It's easy and light, a way to pass time as we wait for the storm to move out.

Except three hours later, we're still fucking waiting.

"We gotta call this," Axel hollers. Finally, a voice of reason.

The wind screams against the tent. My feet now feel soggy inside my jacked-up kicks.

"Let's go," I agree, seconding Axel's point before anyone can argue against it.

Devon swears and shakes his head. "I think you might be right."

"We are," I confirm, jumping into action.

The sooner we can get out of this stupid tent and down the hill, the sooner I can get back to Harper. I need to spend time with my woman, not hang with a bunch of dudes in the middle of nowhere.

Cole frowns but begins to move to take the tent down. "It's just a little rain, Barnes."

"It's fucking cold, Rookie."

River snickers and shifts the weight of his backpack. His eyes turn to Devon. "Next time you want to bond, let's just grab a beer at Corks."

Devon flips him off and I laugh.

Cole pops his head outside of the tent and looks skyward, as if the sun is magically going to beam down on us in the middle of the night.

Without waiting for a response, River and I lead the way out of the tent. We all pack up and then move, slowly in the dark, down the hill, toward the parking lot.

A cold draft beer beats camping any day of the week.

Thursday:
1:04 AM

Me: Want to hear great news? We're heading home early. It seems that the team has bonded enough trying to get the tent to withstand this rainstorm. (Laughing Emoji) I'm not into this, Harper. Please don't ever ask me to go camping.

. . .

6:02 **AM**

Harper: BEST MESSAGE TO WAKE UP TO! Are you home yet? And sorry but I'm not sorry that camping sucked.

8:43 **AM**

Me: Sorry, baby. I passed out the second I got home. I still feel like I didn't sleep enough. Are we on for dinner?

Harper: Welcome back! I'm sorry, I forgot about a happy hour I promised the guys on the team I'd attend. And, since I'm trying to forge more female friendships, I'm hoping a few of their girlfriends join. But one drink, then I'm yours!

I SIGH, trying to stave off my disappointment. I've gotten spoiled, with Harper and me hanging out nearly every day during the summer break. But now that she's caught up in preseason and I'm gearing up for training, our days end later and sometimes we miss each other all together. I know it's just the first week but with us living one floor apart, I didn't think carving out time would be this hard.

I miss Harper so fucking much and...does she really need to attend this happy hour? Can't she go to the next one? Still, it's her job and she's only been there a year. I don't want to give her a hard time since I'm proud of her for loving her work so much. Besides, I know how much she misses having female friends and if some of the Coyotes' significant others are joining along, then it will be good for Harper to go.

. . .

8:47 **AM**

Me: Okay, I'll see you after.

12:42 **PM**

Me: Hey, Coach called a meeting tonight. We're just catching up and watching some game tape. I'm so fucking sorry. And annoyed. I miss you. Call you when I get home.

2:51 **PM**

Harper: Ahhh, that sucks. Of course. Tonight! I'm going to kiss you so hard.

Me: I can't fucking wait.

———

I ADD another weight plate to each end of the bar and get ready to squat. My Apple AirPods are full blast, filling my head with throwback hip-hop instead of the negative thoughts that have been rolling around since my parents' anniversary party. That, coupled with my barely seeing Harper this week, has me in a piss-poor mood.

This week, the distance between us has me rattled. I miss her and it scares me how much I need her. How unsettled I feel with a handful of chirpy text messages as the only communication between us. Harper is the best woman I've ever known and yet, can she really be mine?

Taking her home to meet my family was both a wake-up call and a mistake. A wake-up call because it reminded me just how different the world I hail from is. Just how manipulative my mom can be when proving a point. Just how broken Fiona is in her marriage. Just how off the rails

Charlie has gotten. Except for my dad, who tries his best to hold it all together and put on a brave face, my family has been splintering apart at the seams for years.

And introducing Harper to the Barneses was a mistake. Because it proved how good and pure and generous my girl is. She's not meant to break bread with the Cecilias of my world. She's not built for Charlie's late-night demons. And what kind of a partner will I be in the future? When hockey is over and I have to decide the *after* that my family always brings up?

I fucking hate that Sean Collins is sniffing around again. Has he messaged her this week? Has he tried to intercept her at work? It pisses me off that I don't know because I've barely spoken to her.

After the fucker broke her heart, she shouldn't give him the time of day. And maybe she really isn't. But he clearly knows what he lost. Any man who lost Harper would never fully come back from that. Not unless they got a second chance with the beauty who outshines every other woman.

The distance that's evolved between Harper and me this week has me questioning too many things. It's making me think shit I wouldn't think if I could just wrap her in my arms and kiss her hard.

It has me considering her history with Sean as a threat. Their shared past and similar upbringings has me envisioning their future. And when I do, it's crystal fucking clear. Sean and Harper make sense in ways that Harper and I never will.

I know she doesn't want him. But would she be better off with a man *like* him? Someone from her hometown. A man who wants to stay in Tennessee and build something from the ground up. A man committed to the community, the way she wants to put down roots. A man to experience those thrilling hungry years with, when the future isn't certain, and the money isn't readily available. Does she desire a salt-of-the-earth man who doesn't have a closet filled with ugly family secrets and piles of emotional baggage?

I do an extra set, grunting as my legs begin to fatigue. Training camp kicks off on Monday and yet, I want to burn myself out today. I want to feel too fucking tired to think. Or dwell.

The bar clangs back onto the rack and I step away, reaching for my water bottle. Sweat pours down my spine and my shirt is soaked around my collar and under my arms.

"Hey!" A hand thumps heavily on my back.

I pull an AirPod from my ear and turn, surprised to see Beau Turner. "Hey. What's up, man?"

He tips his chin at me. "Not much. Thought I'd come to The Honeycomb today for a workout. I had breakfast this morning with Gran."

"How's she doing?"

He smirks. "Trying to sign me up for a dance class."

I grin. "Your gran is something else."

"Yeah," he agrees. "How was your weekend in Connecticut?"

I sigh, grabbing a towel and plopping down on a bench. "Amazing and awful," I answer honestly.

Beau sits on a workout bench near mine, his gaze thoughtful. He's a great guy, a solid teammate, but no one on the team is super tight with him. In all fairness, I guess no one is super tight with me either, but I can give off the illusion of closeness.

Beau Turner keeps to himself in a different way. As a veteran, having served in Afghanistan as well as embassy duties, he's loyal, honest, and considerate. He's also quiet, introspective, and struggling. The dark shadows that pass through his eyes, the way he's sometimes lost in thought, mentally in a different place, speaks to experiences no one else on the team fully understands.

He doesn't badmouth anyone. He doesn't make promises he can't keep. He doesn't boast or wager or drink too much. He never brings around women or has a flavor of the week. No, Beau Turner is the kind of man other men emulate, even when they don't know his full story. He's the kind of guy you can confide in, even if he never reciprocates.

"Things with Harper changed?" he guesses, alluding to our unfinished conversation during the hike.

It's on the tip of my tongue to make a joke, to reach for humor, to blow off the concern in his gaze. But something about Beau's expression, about how much he seems to care about my response, about *me*, causes me to share the truth. "I care about her," I mutter, taking a swig of water. "More than care about her."

"And your family?"

I half smile. "She charmed my dad. My mom, well, that's another story." I sigh. "My siblings are both experiencing some big, life-changing issues." I don't elaborate but with Beau, I don't have to. He's perceptive enough to read between the lines.

"So are you," Beau comments.

I look up sharply. I'm nothing like Charlie or Fiona. And yet, I'd be lying if I didn't admit that Fiona's words got to me. *If you love her, Damien, let her go.*

Beau tilts his head. "You've changed since you met Harper. I've seen you more than any of the guys this summer and I promise, they've all noticed a difference in

you. You're more open. You share more. You're less guard-
ed." He shrugs.

"That's not a good thing."

"Why not?"

I blow out a sigh, grasp the back of my neck. I fucking
hate conversations like these and yet, Beau isn't making it
awkward. "I'm leaving myself wide open, man."

"To get hurt?"

I nod.

He smirks. "You think you can be in any type of real
relationship—romantic, platonic, familial—and not be open
to that? It's part of the territory. Otherwise, it's more surface
than real."

I swallow as his words slam into me. He's right. I'm not
really close with anyone *except* Harper. The things I've
shared with her I wouldn't even tell Fiona or Charlie.
Fiona was more embarrassed that I witnessed her
exchange with Gary more than she was about Gary's
cheating.

If you love her, Damien, let her go.

Would I end up disappointing, or worse, hurting
Harper? Would she be better off with someone else?

"Her ex is sniffing around again," I toss out, pissed off
that Sean is on the periphery of her life. Wanting to know
what Beau thinks about it.

"So? Is she engaging him or shutting it down?"

"Shutting it down."

He grins. "You can't be mad at her for being a beautiful,
thoughtful woman. I saw this shit with my sister and man,
Bea's ex drives me nuts. But I couldn't really blame him for
wanting to make things right with her, you know?"

"Yeah," I mutter, seeing his point even though I don't
want to.

"What's really holding you back, man?" Beau cuts to the heart of the matter. "Because these sound like excuses."

"It's not going to last," I murmur, my voice cracking.

Beau frowns. "Why not?"

"Because nothing good ever lasts," I remind him, knowing it's the truth. I've never witnessed a relationship from anyone in my age group, from my generation, that's been able to make it work for the long haul.

After the honeymoon phase ends, I've only seen the cheating, the gambling, the alcohol and drugs. I've known about the other women, witnessed the crushed families, and ached for the broken homes of small children. I've heard my parents' arguments and while they've managed to make it work, they're from a different generation. They're old school. Their betrayals and faults would never survive a relationship today.

"You don't truly believe that..." Beau studies me.

"Harper's pure, Beau. She's a good woman."

"Then be a good man," he volleys.

"Yeah," I say, agreeing with his point even though I don't know how to commit to that. How do you be exactly what your partner needs forever? Through all the changes and ups and downs? How do you not fuck it up?

If you love her, Damien, let her go.

"But the long distance," I throw out. "That would be tough."

"You haven't been traded."

I sigh and stare tight at Beau. "What if I stop making her happy?"

He straightens, leans forward, and stares right at me. His eyes flare with understanding. "You're overthinking this, Barnes. Take it one day at a time and address challenges as they come up, without letting them grow into something bigger. Don't throw up walls where there should be doors."

I nod, knowing that Beau's making valid points. Yet all I can see is Fiona's tear-streaked face. All I hear is Mom's remarks about landing a husband and raising children. Dad's offer about joining the family company.

Could a man who belongs to a family like that truly make a woman like Harper happy? Could I really be enough for the love that she effortlessly gives? Or will I only end up ruining a beautiful, thoughtful woman?

If you love her, Damien, let her go.

————

AFTER A GRUELING WORKOUT WITH TURNER, I call it a day and head home. It's nearly evening by the time I shower, order some dinner, and check my phone to see if Harper messaged.

Harper: Hey! Grabbing drinks with the team now. Bonding and all that jazz. See you after?

Me: Have fun. Yes! Call me for a ride.

I wait fifteen minutes for a reply, but it never comes. Feeling slightly defeated, which is stupid since I know she's busy with work, I pour a drink and head to the balcony. For most of last year, Harper would eventually make an appearance on her balcony. Sometimes, it was with a drink in hand. Other nights, when the temperature dipped, with a tea or hot chocolate. And some of my favorite evenings were when she unrolled a yoga mat and worked through a practice in nothing but tight-ass leggings and a flimsy sports bra.

But tonight, she's out and her balcony is quiet. Empty.

Fuck, I miss her, and it's only been a few days since we ate ice cream and joked around. Is this how the entire season will be? With me longing for her while she makes great strides in her career?

My phone rings and I grin, thinking it's Harper but when Dad's name flashes across the screen, I groan.

"Hey," I answer.

"Damien, good." His voice is clipped.

My disappointment morphs into concern. "What's wrong?"

"Charlie's been arrested."

"What?" I stand up and walk back inside, begin to pace my living room. "For what?"

"DUI. Fucking idiot," Dad mutters. In the background, I hear his fingers clacking away at a keyboard. "I'm pulling some strings, getting him out."

"Of course," I say, trying to keep the sarcasm form my tone. The Barnes family are master puppeteers when it comes to pulling strings. "What do you need?"

Dad clears his throat. "Your brother's hurting and I'm going to get him the help he needs. But, I'm calling about Fiona."

"Okay..." Does he know that Gary cheated on her? Does he know about Gabby? Did something else happen?

"She's here."

"Okay."

"She and Garrett arrived a few hours ago, bags in hand."

I close my eyes and try not to smile. "She's leaving him."

"Your mother—"

"Don't let Mom talk Fiona into staying with Gary. He's a fuckwad and—"

"Prepared the guest suite," Dad finishes his statement and I breathe out a sigh of relief.

"She's really leaving him." I smile.

"Your mom had her doubts but once Fiona mentioned

Gabby..." Dad trails off. "Well, it will be tough for Gary to find work, or a social network, going forward."

"Good."

"Fiona's staying with us for the foreseeable future. When she's ready, I offered her Gary's position."

I chuckle, so fucking happy and relieved to hear this news. "Good," I say again, walking in circles around my house. "I can come home right now, if you need me."

"You start training next week," Dad reminds me.

"I don't care."

"I do," Dad replies. "I know we've been hard on you, Damien. But out of everyone, I'm the proudest of you."

I pull up short. I must have heard that wrong. "What?"

Dad sighs. "You're the only one of my kids who followed your heart. Cultivated your own interests and dreams and went after them. You're the only one who can stand on your own two feet. Like a man. And I'm proud of you for that."

"I, uh..." I scratch the back of my neck, caught so off guard I can't respond. I clear my throat. "Thank you, Dad. That—it means a lot."

"Should've fucking said it sooner. But your mother wants you home. Working for the company."

"Yeah," I say, knowing exactly what Mom wants. And Mom always gets what Mom wants.

"Just...play your heart out this season."

I sigh out a breathless laugh.

"And when you're ready for what's next, the whole company, everything, is yours for the taking."

"Dad?" I ask, wanting to know that I heard him correctly.

"Fiona probably deserves it more than you," he murmurs, as if he's forgotten I'm on the line, "but you're the only one who can fully handle it. I trust you, Damien."

"I—thanks, Dad."

"I trust you," he repeats. Then, "I'm going to post bail for your brother now. We'll get him into a private rehab facility. Should've fucking done that sooner too but we didn't want to make waves."

No, *Mom* didn't want to make waves...but I don't say that. I don't say anything.

"I'll call tomorrow to check on Fiona," I say. "FaceTime with Garrett."

"Yes, please do. That would be good. Good night, Damien."

"Night, Dad." I hang up the phone.

I resume walking aimlessly around my apartment, grappling with my emotions, trying to make sense of my conversation with Dad. This past week, too many things have shifted.

My feelings for Harper. Our relationship.

My relationship with Dad. My understanding of Fiona. The demons Charlie battles.

The future. What do I want? Deep down, I've always wanted the tight-knit family that Beau Turner has, that Harper talks about. If I take over the company, could I help create those familial bonds? Could Fiona, Charlie, and I grow Dad's vision with me at the helm?

He wants to give me the company because he *trusts* me.

Confused and overwhelmed, I head back to my balcony, look down for Harper. But her unit is still dark, her balcony empty. I sigh and sink back into my chair, staring at Harper's place, mentally willing her lights to come on.

I don't want to bother her but tonight, fuck tonight I really need her. I need someone to help me process my thoughts, these swirling emotions. She's the only one I'd ever confide in about my family.

Me: Hey, Harp, how's the bar? You need a ride?

A response never comes. At eleven PM, I turn in for the night, having committed to an early morning run with Beau.

In the morning, I feel defeated that she never replied. Never called. Never came up to my place, even though she has the elevator code.

Is she troubled about the weekend with my family too? Is she second-guessing things? Second-guessing me?

Or is she just exhausted from her first week of preseason and sleeping off a few too many drinks?

The fact that I'm filled with uncertainty bothers me. It fills me with a sense of foreboding and makes me want to shut down. To erect the walls Beau warned me away from.

Blowing out a sigh, I toss on a T-shirt and shorts. Then, I meet Beau and a very grumpy Axel for an early morning run and workout.

When Axel mentions being Maisy and Mila's designated driver and giving Harper a ride home from the bar, my head nearly snaps off my neck. She never called me. She never came over.

She's pulling away, just like I knew she would.

SEVENTEEN
HARPER

MY HEAD POUNDS when I force my eyes open in the morning. I glance at the little clock next to my bed. Shit, it's already afternoon. Closing my eyes, I faceplant into my pillow and let the memories of last night roll over me.

The Coyotes forcing me to join them for a drink. One drink since preseason has officially started.

But one drink turned into more when Coyotes player, and general fan favorite, Cohen Campbell showed up with Mila Lewis and Maisy Stratford. Apparently, the Thunder-bolts captain Devon Hardt and wicked defensemen Axel Daire are dating the Coyote players' longtime friends. Two women I just happen to remember from high school even though they were two grades ahead of me. If I'm being honest, it worked out even better than if some of the Coyotes' girlfriends had joined.

The minute our introductions were made, we found a corner of the bar and our conversation flowed easier than the endless mojitos we consumed. I had promised Damien I'd bounce after one drink but when I tried to leave, Mila convinced me to stay for one more. That easily turned into several.

Eventually, Leo called it a night and reminded me to hit Damien up for a ride home. But I was having so much fun hanging out with women my own age, who grew up in towns similar to mine, with overlapping pasts, that I didn't want to bother Damien. I wanted to stay out, drinking and laughing. I wanted to hold on to this feeling of belonging, of knowing that my place is right here, in Tennessee.

Then, my phone died. When Maisy called Axel to pick her and Mila up, they offered me a ride home and I gratefully accepted. I planned to message Damien and apologize for messing up our plans before I slept, but clearly, I fell asleep before hitting send.

Now, my eyes are crusty, my hair is a tangled bird's nest, and I need water. Ibuprofen. Greasy French fries and a Coke. In any order.

"Shit," I mutter as I force myself into a seated position. My head throbs and my vision swims. Am I still drunk? I squint at my phone.

Damien: Hey, Harp, how's the bar? You need a ride?

Damn. I must have missed that. No new messages since Damien's text from last night and it's almost 1 PM. Is he annoyed with me? Worried?

Ugh, I need a shower.

A knock sounds on my door, loud and obnoxious. A flutter of hope travels through my body. Is it Damien? I'm not exactly disappointed that I didn't see him last night given the shape I woke up in. But it would have been nice to fool around drunk on mojitos and high on him.

The knock sounds again.

"I'm coming," I call out, my voice hoarse, weak,

hungover as fuck. I stop in front of the hall mirror and blanche at my reflection. "I look like utter shit."

Another knock.

Sighing, I tuck some random strands of hair behind my ears and pull open the door, hoping Damien doesn't run when he sees me.

Instead of my sexy boyfriend who I'm missing like crazy, Leo thrusts a green smoothie in my face.

"Don't you have camp?" I ask.

"I already had a four-hour session," he replies, wrinkling his nose at me. "I've got two hours before I'm due back on the field. Don't you have work?"

I wave a hand. "I took a personal day. I wanted to surprise Damien and do something fun before his camp starts next week."

Leo snorts. "How's that working out for you?"

I glare at him, taking the green smoothie and slurping it. "You didn't think to bring me fries?"

He laughs. "This is better. You need to hydrate and get some green in your system."

Meh, debatable. Instead of pushing it, I follow Leo into my living room. He looks around.

"What?" I ask.

"Where's Damien?" He holds up a coffee cup. "I figured he'd be here."

"Oh," I say. "Well, he's not."

Leo frowns. "What did he say when he picked you up? Was he pissed that all the football players were flirting with you?"

I snort. "That was harmless, and you know it."

Leo grins.

"And I got a ride."

"What? Why?" he presses, his frown morphing into a slash of concern.

I wave a hand. "It was late, and my phone died."

"You were drunk. The three of you. Got a ride with whom? Didn't Hardt or the other guy, the brawler—"

"Axel."

"Yeah, him. Didn't one of them come get you girls?"

"Yes." I laugh, shaking my head before I wince. "That hurts. The sun is too bright."

Leo rolls his eyes.

"Axel came to pick us up."

Leo whistles. "Damien is not going to like that."

I force myself to drink more of the smoothie. "Why not? Axel's his teammate," I remind him.

"Yeah, but he doesn't even know you were out drinking with his friends last night."

"What? Mila and Maisy are—"

"Bolts girls. Even though the Coyotes still try to claim them from time to time. You know, because Mila used to date—"

"Avery Callaway," I mutter, squinting as if that will help me recall hazy high-school memories. "She didn't even mention him last night."

Leo shrugs. "She's really happy with Devon Hardt."

"Right."

"But Mila and Maisy are still tight with Cohen so..."

"So, they hang with the Coyotes *and* the Bolts."

"Exactly," Leo confirms.

"So last night, I was hanging out with Damien's friends, and he has no idea."

"Not unless you or one of his friends told him," Leo surmises, drinking the extra coffee. "Hence, why I'm surprised he's not here."

As if on cue, another knock sounds on the door.

Another flutter of hope, another reminder that I look like death, and I pull the door open.

Damien stands on the other side looking rakishly handsome. His eyes drink me in with worry, scanning my entire body once before meeting my eyes. "You okay?"

"Yeah. I'm fine," I croak.

"Glad you're here, man." Leo stands and moves toward us, tugging on my hair playfully.

I yelp because, "I haven't taken Advil yet."

Leo chuckles, clasps Damien on the upper arm, and exits. "See you later, Harp."

"Thanks for the smoothie," I grumble.

Damien's lips pinch at the corners and he frowns, closing the door behind us. Instead of moving into my apartment, he rests his back against the front door, crosses his arms over his chest, and studies me. "You didn't call for a ride."

"Huh?" I peer up at him, trying to follow the conversation.

He swallows and his eyes flash, dark and pained and filled with regret. "I heard from Axel that you were out with the girls, that he took you home."

"Yeah." I lift my eyebrows, waiting for him to get to the point.

"You didn't call me."

"It was late."

"I'm your man," he says it like a reminder. Like he somehow failed me. "And we had plans. Dinner."

"I know." I shake my head. "I'm sorry about that. That was my fault, and I should have messaged you earlier. My phone died."

"I've barely seen you this week," he bites out, frustration heavy in his tone.

"Preseason started." I squint at him, note the tension rolling off his broad shoulders, read the desperate plea in his eyes. "I know I messed up and I'm sorry but...either I'm still drunk or something is seriously off because I don't understand what's happening right now."

Damien pushes off the door and rakes a hand through his hair, agitated. "Why didn't you call me?" His tone is accusatory.

"Look, I'm sorry you're upset. I never intended that; next time, I'll call you for a ride."

"I didn't know you were with my friends."

"Okay," I say slowly, wondering if I embarrassed him somehow. As I wrack my mind for something I may have said last night, I realize I don't recall much. Shit, how much did I drink?

"We just, we haven't been on the same page this week."

He's right. I've felt the distance too, disguised behind cutesy text messages, which is why I took today off. But I don't tell him that. Instead, I say, "We're both getting busy at work; we knew this was coming. We're supposed to figure it out. Together. Is that what we're doing?" I cross my arms over my chest. The gesture is protective, as if my body senses what's coming before my mind catches up.

Throughout this week, I've felt Damien pulling away. It was slow and subtle; sometimes I questioned if I was imagining it all. But now that he's standing in my apartment rattling off words I never pictured him saying, I realize he's withdrawing.

He stares at me for a long moment, his breath coming faster than it was a moment ago. His eyes are unfathomable, dark and swirling one second and flat and placid the next. "I don't know," he says finally.

I flinch, as if his words packed a physical blow. In a way, they did. "What?" I grapple with the realization that he's putting up a shield. "You...you don't know what? If we're still doing this?" I gesture between us. "Us?"

Pain streaks across his expression like a shooting star. If I had blinked, I would have missed it. "This is harder than I thought," he admits, yanking at his hair. He turns away from me, walks to pace, and turns back. "The demands of our schedules, the upcoming season...I need to focus on hockey."

"Have I ever asked you to not do that?"

"I didn't even know where you were last night. Or with whom," he tosses back.

I roll my eyes. "I told you I was getting drinks with the Coyotes."

"Yeah, with the football team," he bites out.

"Sorry, I didn't realize you were going to go all overprotective boyfriend on my ass the second I—"

"I care about you, Harper," he cuts me off, his eyes hardening. "I care about you a lot. But I'm not cut out for this." Now he's the one gesturing between us.

I work a swallow, my bravado slipping. Instead, tears are gathering in the corners of my eyes and my throat is tightening painfully.

At my unchecked emotion, Damien's facade begins to crumble. "Harper." He reaches for me, but I step back, out of his embrace. His face falls. "You deserve more than what I can give."

"Why could you give it a week ago and not now? What changed?" My voice cracks as all the awkwardness from the weekend with his family floods my mind. "Is this about your family? Because I'm a big girl, Damien. I can meet with a stylist and—"

"You shouldn't have to." His voice is hard but quiet. It lacks anger or hurt and instead, holds a monotone quality I don't know how to process. "You're perfect the way you are."

"So perfect you don't want to be with me?"

He shakes his head, reaching out to cup my cheek. "I'm the issue, Harper, not you."

"Original," I snort.

He drops his hand. "This was never going to work."

"You're looking for excuses."

"Maybe," he admits. And fuck, how the hell am I supposed to argue that? How am I supposed to fight for something when my opponent, the man I thought was my partner, has already thrown in the towel?

"Why are you doing this, Damien? Why?" Tears leak over my eyelids and stream down my cheeks. I'm too much of a mess—physically and emotionally—to wick them away.

Damien does it for me, brushing my tears off my cheeks with gentle, steady hands. "It's better now, before we get in too deep."

"I'm already in deep." My voice cracks again and I hate how fucking weak I'm being. I swore I wouldn't do this again. After Sean, I swore I'd wisen up; I'd be too formidable to let a man crack me and yet, right now, it feels like a crater just took out my heart.

You're good for him, Harper. Grace's words come back to haunt me.

I know! I want to scream. *But right now, is he good for me?*

"Trust me, it would have been worse by Thanksgiving."

I reach for some leverage and manage a sneer. "Skiing in Aspen?"

Damien doesn't take the bait. Instead, he drags his thumb along my cheekbone. "Thank you for this summer, Harper. I'll never forget it."

I close my eyes, defeated. Hurt. Aching and empty.

Damien's kiss on my forehead is featherlight and then, he's gone. The door closes with a soft snick, and I'm left in my apartment, with the sunlight streaming in, the birds chirping outside, and a gaping hole in my chest.

Damien Barnes came into my life like a tornado, sweeping me and everything up in his orbit. And he left just as quickly, with a path of destruction and devastation in his wake.

I blow out a deep breath and force myself to take a shower. There, my tears mingle with the water, and I dig deep for the armor I used to wear.

I allow myself my shower to wail and wallow. But when I step out and dry off, I cloak myself in fortitude.

I will not crumble because a man doesn't want me.

I will not break because Damien Barnes rejected me.

Instead, I'll build the community I want to be part of and tell men to fuck right off.

Because I, Harper Henderson, don't need anyone but myself.

I am *more* than enough.

EIGHTEEN
DAMIEN

IT'S my first day of training camp and I'm dragging. Physically lagging and mentally all over the damn place.

Coach Merrick blows a whistle. "I know you had a fun summer, but gentlemen, what the hell is going on? You look like a high-school team instead of the Thunderbolts."

Coach Scotch echoes him. "Line up."

The team forms a straight line on the ice.

The coaches stare at us, their gazes hard. "We're going to run drills for the next two hours. After that, everyone take the afternoon and figure out how to come back mentally committed and locked in to perform for tomorrow. This is the only reprieve you will get this season. But we are not starting the season on this shitty note. So, get your shit together." Coach Scotch's eyes settle on me, hard and unyielding.

I bite the corner of my mouth and give a small nod.

Coach Merrick blows the whistle.

The next two hours are fucking hell. Torture. I sweat profusely, my conditioning subpar. My body aches from too much time away from the ice. I feel slow, my brain in some type of fog.

I nearly weep with relief when the final whistle blows, signaling the end of the session.

"You okay?" Beau asks.

I nod, pulling off my helmet.

His eyes are shadowed with worry. "What's going on?"

"Called it quits with Harper," I admit.

He heaves out a sigh. "You think that was the right call?"

"It wasn't going to work." I skate off the ice with him beside me.

"You sabotaged it."

I snort. "I tend to do that."

Beau swears and I glare at him. "If you love her, truly love her, then she deserves your best."

If you love her, Damien, let her go.

"And I know that your best is better than this," Beau tacks on, exiting the ice before me. "Do better, Barnes."

I stare at his receding back, wondering how the hell he can read me when most people don't bother to look past the easy smile and joking remarks.

"Barnes," Coach Scotch interrupts my thoughts.

I exit the ice. "Yes, Coach?"

"You good?"

"Yes."

"Summer was good?" he presses.

"All's good," I say, unwilling to go deeper.

Coach knows I'm bullshitting him, but he nods slowly, not forcing the issue. "Whatever's going on, sort it out before tomorrow. If you give me that shit performance on the ice again, like you're not even trying, I'll call up Carpenter." He references the second string left wing.

Damn, that fucking hurt to hear.

"I understand," I clip out.

"Good." Coach Scotch walks in the other direction as I make my way toward the locker room.

I feel like shit, mostly from Harper. Mostly from missing her so goddamn much. But also because I don't like letting my team down. I don't like letting myself down. I need to get my shit together.

I swear to myself that by tomorrow, I'll have my emotional crap locked down. This isn't like me. I don't rattle. I don't carry my personal issues onto the ice. I shut things down, smile through the pain, and perform.

I push into the locker room and make my way to my locker. But my hand freezes on the door when I hear Harper's name.

"Yeah, with Mila and Harper," Axel's saying. "All I'm good for these days is being DD. That's twice in one week." He laughs.

Devon snorts. "Mila was hungover as hell. Again."

Again? Are they talking about last week or last night? Guilt swarms through me for how I reacted last week. My girl went out and got drunk with friends, new friends, and I snapped at her. Even when I know how much it means for her to form new friendships with women in her age group. Yeah, she should have messaged me but was I really that upset over a missed takeout dinner?

No, I was agonizing over how hard it was to miss her. Over how difficult the transition to balancing a relationship with our busy work schedules is. Over all the uncertainty and challenges waiting in our future.

And now, I'm in a hell of a lot more agony.

I hang my head. At least Harper's hanging out with

great people. Mila and Maisy are two of the best women I know.

"Mila said there was some trouble with the ex," Devon comments.

Fuck. I stop breathing. Sean Collins showed up there? If Harper is hurting half as badly as I am, did she react emotionally? Did she talk to him? Or worse, allow him to comfort her? Did he take advantage of her emotional state?

Nausea churns in my stomach and my hand clenches the locker door hard. I want to simultaneously vomit and rip the door off its hinges.

I feel inconsolable and desperate. Out of control and reckless.

Shit, is this how Charlie felt when Felicity stepped out on him? Is this feeling the one he chases away with drugs, booze, and other women? Is that what he meant by coping?

"Ah, fucking Josh," Axel mutters and I recognize the name as Maisy's ex-boyfriend. Relief filters through my veins and I begin to breathe out a sigh of relief. "Nah, it wasn't him. It was Harper's ex. What's his name again, Damien?" Axel glances at me. "You must have put him in his place by now, huh?"

A new emotion barrels through me. Fear. What the fuck happened last night? Why would I have to put Sean in his place?

At my expression, Axel swears and Devon looks up.

"What happened with Harper?" Axel asks.

"We broke up," I mutter.

"Mila didn't fucking tell me that," Devon says.

"She's a better secret keeper than you," Axel taunts him.

"Fuck off. Maisy didn't tell you either," Devon spits back.

Axel tips his head in agreement. Then, his narrowed eyes swing toward me. "It explains why she was so drunk."

"And crying," Devon mutters. "I thought it was a family thing."

I snort and it's painful. "Yeah, maybe because of *my family*."

"What's going on?" Axel tries again.

I sigh. "It wasn't going to work."

Devon narrows his eyes, pinning me with a hard look. "Why not? Because you've got money and—"

"Because my future is uncertain," I cut him off.

He fucking laughs. "Are you shitting me? All our futures are fucking uncertain. Any one of us could be traded at any minute."

I close my eyes, bang my head back against the locker door. Devon must signal some shit to the other guys because little by little, everyone filters out except for Devon, Axel, and Beau. "Our schedules are busy. Things are too hectic."

This time, Axel laughs. "Tell me something I don't fucking know, Barnes."

I stare at the guys, taking time to study each of them. "Eventually, I would have fucked it up. You were right"—I glance at Axel—"hurting her would be so much worse than feeling my own pain. Eventually, my family and I and the world I come from, it would have fucking destroyed her."

The guys are quiet for a long minute before Axel shakes his head. "I didn't mean it like that. I meant for you to man up and be the kind of guy she deserves."

"What if I'm not good enough?" My deepest fear cuts the air like a confession.

Devon's face twists and Beau respectfully averts his gaze.

"That's the dumbest shit I've ever heard, Barnes,"

Devon says. "Sure, you don't let people in easily. But fuck, man, from what I've seen and heard of you and Harper, you were trying. Don't even pretend like you didn't go all in with her this summer."

"He did," Axel answers for me.

Beau nods in agreement.

"And then, I hurt her," I remind them.

"You love her?" Beau asks.

I roll my lips together. "Yeah."

"Then do whatever it takes to be the man she deserves. The man *you* want her to be with. Not the man you think she wants. Because she wants you. She already chose you, Damien. You're the one who threw up walls. You're the one who backed away instead of talking to her." He reminds me of our conversation from last week.

I scrape a palm along my jawline. "Maybe it's better this way."

Axel shrugs. "If you don't want to work for it? Then yeah, it is. Let her go. Let her find someone better, a man willing to put in the work to deserve her."

I cut him a look and he smirks. "Beau is right. If you love her, be the man you want her to be with. That guy is more than enough."

"What if it's too late?" I ask, hoping like hell it isn't.

Devon slaps my shoulder. "Then you didn't try hard enough. Some things in life, Damien, don't come with a silver spoon. You gotta earn them."

"Fuck off." I flip him my middle finger.

He snickers. "Get her back. You were happier with her."

"I know," I admit. With Harper, I was truly happy.

Shame and guilt roll through me. I messed this up so

fucking badly. Just the way I told her I would, like a self-fulfilling prophecy.

Why would she take me back? Why would she give me a second chance? I pumped the brakes before we ever had a chance to truly take a joy ride. Because I got scared and overwhelmed.

Because I wasn't enough.

"You're enough, Barnes," Beau says quietly. "But you have to believe that you are."

The guys leave me alone in the locker room and I sit in the quiet for a long-ass time. I try to sort out my shit. I want to be with Harper.

Fuck, I need her. I miss her. I fucking love her.

The realization dawns with perfect clarity and I feel like an idiot for never telling her the words. For never proving to her their meaning.

My phone rings and I pick up.

"Dad?"

"Hi, Damien. How's training camp?"

"Brutal," I admit.

Dad laughs, like he enjoys the thought of me busting my ass. Hell, maybe he does. "How's Harper?"

I swallow against the lump in my throat. Is this the fucking day that I need to admit my fuck-ups to the entire world? "We're...we broke up."

Dad sighs. "I like her, Damien."

"I love her, Dad." My hands shake as I admit the words out loud, again. To my dad instead of Harper.

"I know," Dad says.

"You do?"

"Yeah. I could tell the second you first spoke about her. Your voice changed. She's a good woman, Damien. If you can fix it..."

"You think it's my fault?"

"Or mine," he admits.

"What?" I ask, trying to follow our conversation.

"Your mom and I did our best, but we could have done better. Too many times, I capitulated to your mother's demands because it was easier than fighting. I didn't put in the work to balance things, to make our relationship thrive. And that's the example I left for you."

"Dad, you've always been a lot more down-to-earth, understanding and considerate, hell, even supportive, than Mom."

"Maybe to you. But not always toward her. Damien, relationships are hard. They take work. Continuous effort and care. Like trying to grow a garden. If you love Harper, you need to nurture that love."

"And what about the future? The company? After hockey?"

Dad chuckles. "Ah, son. I'll sell the whole thing and wash my hands of it if it means my children will be happy."

"What?" I sputter. Is he serious?

"My whole life, I wanted to build something I could be proud of. A legacy. But as I got older, I realized my legacy, my true legacy, is you, Fiona, and Charlie. These last few years..." Dad sighs heavily. "These last few years, I've watched you all spiral. I've watched you run to Europe and then Tennessee. I've watched Fiona lose pieces of herself to Gary, and Charlie succumb to the lure of drugs and alcohol. It changes things, seeing your kids struggle. It changed me."

"You'd really sell the company?"

"In a heartbeat," he says without hesitation. "I don't want you or your siblings to take a job because it's easy. Or you think you're supposed to. I want you to hunger for something, to work for it. That goes for careers and relationships. You may lose the woman you love because you don't know how to reconcile your relationship with her with the world you were raised in. Your sister just started divorce proceedings. Charlie's in rehab. The future can be whatever the three of you want it to be but you've gotta make those choices. You have to make that future happen."

I work a swallow as he lays it out, piece by piece. All the mistakes and failures, all the hurt and betrayals.

"When I was young, I thought if I had money, it would solve all my problems," Dad continues. "And I wouldn't have any. But you know what, Damien? Everyone has problems. Everyone has challenges. It's how you address them that makes a legacy. And I'm not very proud of the one I currently have. I'd rather you be happy, Fiona be whole, and Charlie be healthy than have a company with my name on it."

Silence stretches between us as I glance around the empty locker room and try to understand my dad's words.

"Dad—"

"If you want it, it's yours. I believe in your ability to make it better than I did. I believe in you, Damien. These past few years, you've really shown what you're capable of. But if you don't want it, if you want to settle down in Tennessee with Harper, then you should do that too. Always choose love and happiness over money and expectation."

"How did you do both? The company and Mom? I mean, thirty-five years is a big deal, Dad."

"Yeah." Dad chuckles. "But I didn't really do both, Damien. I ran the company and Mom ran the household. Mom raised you. You may not remember it now, but when you three were kids, I was never home. I was always working, always grinding, and Mom held us all together. That's why she expects so much. She doesn't want you to have to work so hard to find stability."

I frown, seeing his point, seeing my mom in a new light.

"But anything meaningful takes work," Dad continues. "So, if you want Harper..."

"I've got to put in the work."

"Yep," Dad says.

I shake my head. It's unbelievable that Dad and I are having this conversation. That he's giving me advice. That I'm taking it.

"I always thought you weren't proud of me," I admit.

Dad clucks, making a sound I don't understand. "I'm sorry you felt that way, son. I've always been proud. I just didn't put in the work our relationship needed."

"And you are now."

"If you'll let me."

"I'd like that."

"Me too," he says. "Now, go win back your girl and let me know if you need any advice. I did build a hedge maze you know."

I snort, that stupid maze finally making sense. "Thanks, Dad."

"Talk to you soon, Damien."

I end the call and blow out an exhale.

What the hell is happening to my family? What the hell is happening in my life? Dad would really sell the company?

The first person I want to share the news with, the breakthrough that my dad and I are growing closer, confiding in each other, is Harper.

And that realization is everything.

I love her so damn much. I will not lose the only woman I've ever loved.

NINETEEN

HARPER

"TO THE FIRST game of the preseason," Mila lifts her margarita.

"Congrats, Cohen." Maisy follows suit. Leo clears his throat and Maisy ducks her head, blushing. "Sorry. Congrats to the Coyotes!"

A cheer rings out through Corks, the Coyotes' regular hangout bar. And now, also the Thunderbolts' go-to place. Apparently, it used to be riddled with tension but over the past year, the teams have mingled more, and now, even some Bolts players are here to celebrate the Coyotes' win.

"That was one hell of a catch," I say to Leo, knowing that his final touchdown changed the outcome of the game. He scored with less than one minute on the clock to break the tie and ensure a Coyotes victory.

He gives me a grateful grin. "Thanks, Harp."

"You grow up on football too?" Axel asks me.

"Hell yeah," I laugh. "I'm from here, remember? The Coyotes are—"

"The pride and joy of Southern football," a bunch of people chant.

Devon snickers as Axel glances around the space, bewildered. "Right," he agrees.

The door to Corks opens and Beau and Bea Turner walk in. Cole slides off his barstool to meet his girlfriend and her brother. It's sweet, watching the Bolts teammates interact. It makes me miss Damien. Is he coming? Does he know I'm here? Would he stay away to avoid seeing me?

Or worse, is he pissed off that I'm hanging out with his friends again? Although, to be fair, it's by default, given the Coyotes/Bolts overlap at Corks.

The door to the bar opens again and my hope bubbles up. Shit. It sinks real fast when I note Sean. I duck lower in my barstool, causing Devon to glance over his shoulder. He glowers when he sees my ex.

"This guy does not back off, does he?" Devon mutters.

Avery Callaway, the Coyotes QB, overhears and glances at Sean. When his eyes meet mine, they hold an edge of sympathy. "Not when he knows what he's lost," he murmurs. His eyes dart from mine to Mila and back again.

Devon turns, his jaw twitching, but the bartender intercedes, asking Avery what he's drinking.

Mila shoots me an understanding glance and I sigh, knowing what's coming. Sean spots me and walks closer. As he does, some of the Bolts and Coyotes players pull rank, shifting closer to me.

It should be comical, these big, tough athletes willing to intervene on my behalf. Instead, it fills my entire being with warmth. I've waited a long time to be part of a group, to feel accepted, to have a community in Tennessee again. Right now, with players from both teams lending their support, letting me know that they've got my back, I could cry.

God, I wish Damien were here. If he was, none of their show would be necessary. He would shut down Sean in an instant. But he's not here because he doesn't want to do this with me. He doesn't want to be an us.

So, I'll tell Sean, again, that we don't have a future. That I've moved on. That I don't want to keep having the same conversation since the outcome will never change.

"Harper." Sean stops in front of me, glancing around nervously at the hard eyes and posturing bodies of the Coyotes and Bolts players.

Mila snorts and Maisy hides her smile behind her margarita.

Behind Mila, I catch Beau's frown and Bea's concerned expression.

I sigh and turn back to Sean. No doubt Damien will hear about this awkward exchange. I'm sure he'll wonder if I'm seeing Sean again, if I've moved on from him. Will he care?

Will he be jealous? Or want me back?

God, what is wrong with me that *that* is my thought process?

I'm enough. I'm enough. I'm enough.

"How are you, Sean?" My tone is polite but cool.

He shuffles from one foot to the next. "Uh, could we talk?"

I open my mouth but Cohen cuts in. "You're already talking."

Sean's gaze shoots to him. "I, um, Harp, I'd like to speak *privately*."

Gage, another Coyotes player coming back from an ACL injury, shrugs. "Whatever you have to say to my girl, you can say in front of everyone."

Sean's eyes narrow, his lips flattening into a thin line. "Your girl?" He looks at me. "Are you...dating?"

"Gage is trying," Cohen says smoothly, tossing an arm

around my shoulders. "But everyone knows I'm putting in my best work." Cohen grins at me. Winks. "Right, babe?"

Oh, God. Mila's shoulders shake with laughter and even Axel looks amused.

Avery leans forward on the bar, swipes his thumb over his bottom lip like some male model in an underwear commercial. "But our date, come on, Harp. That was special, right? I mean, that night..."

"Wasn't as beautiful as ours," Cohen continues, batting his long eyelashes at me. I swear, he looks like a Greek god. No wonder fangirls physically fight for his attention.

"From the moment I saw you, Harper, I haven't thought about anyone else," Gage continues, as if Cohen and Avery aren't trying to upstage him.

Leo snorts. "You know Harper and I run together every morning, right?"

"Harper, what the hell is going on?" Sean asks.

Gage slugs an arm around Sean's shoulders, squeezing his neck a little too tightly. "What's going on is that Harper is *our* sweetheart. The whole team fucking loves her. To be honest, half of us are *in love* with her. You blew your wad, man."

Margarita comes out of Maisy's nose.

"Shit," Axel mutters, grabbing her a stack of napkins. He pushes them into her face without taking his eyes off the ridiculous scene unfolding by the bar.

Maisy snorts into the tissues, half laughter and half sob. "Tequila burns."

Cole laughs. Beau pulls out his phone and lifts it to his ear. Bea looks at me curiously.

What the hell is happening? I should put a stop to this; I know I should. But Sean hasn't gotten the hint yet so...is it awful if I let my friends look out for me? After fending for myself for so long, it feels amazing to have people care enough to intercede. The fact that my friends are professional football players certainly doesn't hurt.

I lean into Cohen's touch and his hand slides down my back, tugging on my shirt to encourage me to let this charade play out. But as Sean's cheeks fill with color, I feel bad and intercede.

"Sean, we had a really great relationship in high school. I'm back now and I hope when our paths cross, we can be friendly. But I've moved on. I've met someone—"

"Who?" His eyes dart between the football players, a glower on his face. "Where's the hockey player? Barnes?"

Beau's eyes snap to my face at Damien's name. I see him studying me in my peripheral vision, but I don't turn away from Sean.

Instead, I take a deep breath. Even though it physically hurts to admit it, I say, "Damien changed the game for me, Sean. I won't settle for less than what he made me feel. And, if I'm being honest, no man has ever made me feel like him."

Cohen mock gasps next to me. Gage smacks a hand over his cheek. Avery stifles his laughter.

"You wound me!" Cohen says accusingly.

I shake my head, smiling up at him.

"We really do love you, Harp." Cohen grins.

"And we want to see you happy," Gage adds.

"Always," Leo says.

Avery passes me a drink. I accept it gratefully and glance at Sean.

"The past is the past. I've moved on, Sean."

Slowly, he nods. He looks around at the guys surrounding me. At the new friends I've made in Mila and Maisy. "I hope you find what you're looking for, Harper."

Leaning back against the bar, surrounded by friends who willingly stand up for me, I smile. Even though Damien isn't here, and I desperately wish he was, I also know that what we shared was real. When he promised me that, I know he meant it. "I already have."

The words are freeing, shifting some of the hurt I've been drowning in since Damien pushed me away. This year, I've made a lot of changes in my life. But I evolved, I moved forward, and I'm proud of the roots I'm planting here.

"See you, Harper." Sean turns around and strides out of Corks.

"That was fucking epic," Devon says, grinning at some of the Coyotes.

"You were hilarious," Mila tells Cohen.

Cohen drops a kiss to the crown of my head and orders a round of shots. "This is because I'm drowning in misery from your rejections," he tells me, gesturing toward the row of shot glasses. "Not because we won the game."

I laugh and nod in understanding.

As I turn toward the bar to take a shot, the door opens. I glance over my shoulder and freeze because Damien's eyes zero in on mine. He strides toward me with purpose and my heart rate begins to gallop. Some of the tequila from the shot glass spills onto my hand as Cohen passes it to me and I fumble the little glass.

"Take it quick," Leo says quietly.

And I do. I toss back the tequila, hoping for liquid courage, as the man who hurt me, the one I can't get over, stops in front of me.

All the guys who previously closed ranks shuffle back a few steps.

"Traitors," Mila whispers playfully.

"Shh," Maisy scolds her.

Their eyes are glued to Damien and me. But I can't fully look at anyone because Damien, with his reckless green eyes and smartass smirk, is staring at me like he can't believe I'm really here.

"Dam—"

"I love you, Harper. I'm so fucking in love with you that I can't see straight," he announces it like a declaration and silence falls over Corks.

"Damnnnn," Avery mutters. "That was good, man."

"Shh!" Maisy's voice is louder this time.

"Can we talk?" Damien asks.

"Whatever you have to say—" Gage starts but Leo smacks a hand over his mouth.

Devon snickers.

I roll my eyes but allow Damien to take my hand and pull me away from the group.

I'm just hearing him out, I lie to myself.

I don't have to forgive him. He hurt me, deeply. And still, a part of me understands him. A part of me yearns for his apology. For him.

When we step outside the bar, Damien turns to face me.

"I'm sorry."

"For what?" I arch an eyebrow, vowing to not go easy on him.

"For hurting you. For not telling you sooner how I feel. For not manning up and being enough for you."

"You were already enough," I tell him truthfully.

He works a swallow. "I was on my way here. Beau invited me."

I nod.

"But then he told me you were here, and I drove faster."

"Okay."

"And then he called me, when Sean showed up." His nostrils flare. "I heard what you said."

"Shit," I mutter, blushing furiously. Even though it's realistic to think my words would have gotten back to Damien, I didn't realize he heard me say them. That he was...listening in.

"Did you mean it?"

I blow out a breath and square my shoulders. I swore to myself I wouldn't compromise. That I need to be enough, as I am. "Every word," I admit.

Damien's mouth crashes over mine. He kisses me hard, with a reckless, needy, desperate edge. It reminds me of the first night I kissed him, and I snort, pulling back and shaking my head.

"Sorry," he mutters, raking a hand through his hair. "Fuck, Harper. I, please, Harper."

I lift both my eyebrows. Waiting.

Damien drops to his knees.

"Holy shit, is he proposing?" a voice screams from inside Corks.

"Get up!" I tell him, tugging on his arm.

"No." He shakes his head.

"People are going to think you're proposing." I suck in air, borderline hyperventilating. "You're not, right?"

He grins, that annoying smirk I love. "Not yet, sweet girl."

"Damien! People are going to think you're—"

"I only care what you think."

I roll my eyes and plant a hand on my hip. "What do you want to say?"

"I want to grovel. I want to win you back. I want to earn your trust and deserve your love. I want to spend every fucking day manning up for you. I want another chance, Harp. And I want you to know that I pushed you away because I was scared, fucking petrified, that I'd ruin it in the end. That I'd hurt you. That I wouldn't be enough for you. And then, I made all those things come true." His hands clasp mine and squeeze. "I'm sorry."

"You said that already."

"It warrants repetition."

I breathe out a deep exhale, relief flowing through my veins at his apology. "You really hurt me," I tell him honestly.

"I know."

"I love you, Damien."

His eyes shine with hope.

"I never stopped," I continue. "But I don't trust your feelings."

His mouth twists in pain.

"So, you need to prove them," I say, watching his eyes widen in surprise.

"I will. Every fucking day, Harp, I will." He stands and inside Corks, people cheer, even though they have no idea what's transpiring between Damien and me.

"We'll see," I say noncommittally.

"Tell me how you want to handle this. How do we move forward?"

I think about it, rolling my lips together. Damien waits patiently for me to gather my thoughts.

"We should date," I decide.

He laughs, the sound loud and uninhibited and one of his rare laughs he only gives me. "Harper Henderson, would you please, pretty fucking please with all the cherries in the goddamn universe on top, have dinner with me tomorrow night?"

"Tomorrow night already? You want me to give you a Saturday night? I think you need to build up to—"

He cuts me off with another kiss and this time, I kiss him back, letting his tongue tangle with mine. I melt into his strong, solid frame.

Another cheer sounds from Corks. I feel Damien's mouth curve into a smile against mine. "We could be something, Harper," he says, repeating the words from the night we officially met.

"We already are," I say back.

"Hell yeah, we are." Then, he kisses me again.

A kiss that rivals all the others.

TWENTY

DAMIEN

THE ELEVATOR DOORS open and Harper waltzes in. She's holding a bottle of wine, rocking skintight leggings and a crop top. Her hair is piled on top of her head and her face is clear of makeup.

"You look beautiful," I tell her.

She rolls her eyes. "I'm supposed to trust you again, remember?"

I laugh. "That wasn't a line; it was the fucking truth."

Harper rolls her eyes and plants the wine bottle down on my kitchen island. She sits on a barstool. Turning, I grab a stack of takeout containers and line them up in front of her. "We've got poppers—"

"A personal fave."

"And nachos." I open another container. "Mozzarella sticks."

Harper whistles.

"And"—I pop the lid on the final box—"quesadillas."

"This is perfect," she comments, grabbing a quesadilla.

I pour two glasses of wine and pass her one. "Tomorrow night will be fancy."

"Where are you taking me?" Her eyes sparkle.

"Strickland's." I reference the top steakhouse in Knoxville.

She grins but shakes her head. "You don't really have to wine and dine me, you know?"

"I want to. I want to fix so many things." I sigh. "I wish I could go back and not mess it up from the start."

"Me too," she admits.

I study her, watch how she picks at a chunk of melted cheese and pops it into her mouth. "Why are you letting me off so easily?"

She chews thoughtfully. "Honestly, I didn't mean to. I had full intentions of slapping you if you tried to talk to me again."

"Good," I comment dryly.

"I spent that whole weekend crying my eyes out. Got drunk with Mila and Maisy."

Fuck, that hurts to hear. But, "I'm glad you found friends in them."

"Me too. I wracked my brain for every snippet of conversation…" She shakes her head. "I kept trying to figure out what happened. Why did you throw up a wall?"

"What did you decide?" I ask, curious to know what she thinks went wrong.

"That you've never done this before." She shrugs simply. "Things with you were always one step forward, two steps back. We hooked up at my reunion and the next morning, you sent me a text calling me *buddy*." Her nose wrinkles with disgust.

"Shit." I hang my head.

"Whenever we got too close, you pulled back. It was a pattern." She takes a sip of wine. "And it hurt to be on the receiving end of that."

I reach for her hand. "Harper, I'm so fucking—"

She holds up a hand, stopping my apology. "I know. I don't need you to keep apologizing. I need you to let me in. Share your scary with me. Whatever is freaking you out, whatever is making you worry, tell me. Give me a chance to navigate this with you."

I tug her closer and plant a soft kiss on her lips. "I promise."

"And I will do my best to have patience." She smiles.

I laugh.

And then, we eat dinner out of takeout containers and drink late into the night, catching up on the past week, out on my balcony. When it's after midnight, I escort her back to her apartment and kiss her good night.

"See you tomorrow?" she asks.

"I'll knock on your door at 7 PM."

Harper smiles and it's breathtaking. Something shifts in my chest and for the first time since my parents' anniversary party, I feel like I can breathe again. "I'll be ready."

"Good night, sweet girl."

"'Night, Damien."

I wait until I hear the lock on her door slide into place. Then, I go back to my penthouse and clean up the kitchen.

My phone buzzes with a text and I smile when I see my sister's name. I spoke to my nephew earlier, but Fiona and I have been playing phone tag.

Fiona: I'm sorry for what I said about you and Harper when we were at Mom and Dad's house. I was hurting and projected my shit with Gary onto your relationship. I shouldn't have done it, Damien. I hope you get the girl. Harper's really great. My eyes are closing but I'll call you tomorrow. Thanks for FaceTiming with Garrett. You made his day. We love you.

Me: Thanks Fi. I appreciate your saying that. I'm trying my damnedest and I hope I get the girl too. Let's talk tomorrow. Give Garrett a goodnight kiss from me. Love you.

Even though I don't need Fiona's words to know that fighting for Harper is right for me, it's still nice to receive her message. As shitty as her situation with Gary is, it's not my reality with Harper and I'm glad Fiona recognizes it.

Before I call it a night, I dial my dad.

"Damien?" He answers on the first ring.

"Dad, I've got a date tomorrow night."

His laughter rolls through the line, easy and sincere.

"Damien?" my mom's voice sounds through the line.

I pull the phone away from my ear, frowning.

"You're on speaker, son," Dad clarifies.

"Hi, Mom," I say, a little confused.

"Did you get her back?" Mom asks, surprising me further.

"I hope so," I say, telling my parents about where I'm taking Harper for dinner tomorrow night.

"Bring her flowers," Mom suggests.

"I thought you didn't really like Harper," I say, truthfully.

Mom sighs. "I never gave her a chance. Having Fiona living here, we've been talking and...well, your dad spoke to me about the company." Mom lets out a big sigh. "I'm sorry, Damien. It's easy to get caught up in things without truly evaluating them and that's what I did. I had a vision for what I wanted your, Fiona's, and Charlie's lives to look like. I didn't want the three of you to struggle, the way your father and I have."

"And we did for many years, Damien," Dad interjects.

"But I was wrong. And I'm sorry. I hope after Harper gives you another chance, she'll give me one."

"We're coming down for the Rib Shack," Dad reminds me.

I shake my head, truly shocked by this turn of events.

Mom's silent on the other end of the line. Waiting.

I clear my throat. "I'll ask her, Mom, but I'm sure she'll say yes."

Mom lets out the breath she was holding. "I'd like that. If it's okay with you, send me her number. I'd like to call her. Talk to her myself."

Dad coughs in the background to conceal his chuckle.

Smiling, I agree and forward Harper's number to Mom. "Just give it a few days. Let's make sure I can pull off this date."

"You got it," Mom agrees. "I'll let you talk to Dad now."

"Good night, Mom."

"Love you, Damien."

"Love you too," I say, realizing how much I mean the words, even when I haven't said them in years.

Dad comes back on the line. We talk more about my date with Harper, and I don't shoot down any of his suggestions.

———

I'M NERVOUS.

My palms feel clammy. My stomach churns, almost violently. My fingers clasp the bouquet of flowers tightly. I pace the hallway, loitering in front of Harper's door, too nervous to knock.

I never want to take her for granted. I never want to hurt her again.

I don't want to be the kind of man who doesn't know how to treasure the greatest reward in the world—love. I want to be the kind of man, boyfriend, future *husband*, who excels at commitment, who makes Harper feel cherished and special, who gives her the world.

I let out a long exhale and pause in front of her door. This is the first step to moving down that path. Even if Harper doesn't realize it, I'll never not be there for her again.

In her mind, this is our first date. In mine, this is the start of our forever.

I knock on the door.

A few seconds of silence tick by and I grin that she's not waiting for me, that she's going to make me sweat a little.

The door opens and I fall into her deep blue gaze.

"You brought flowers." She smiles as I thrust them into her hands.

"You look beautiful, Harper." I tell her the truth, drinking in the happiness that flares in her eyes. I love that I can make her happy, that I possess the ability to make her feel safe.

I'll never not honor that again.

"And you look very dapper," she says, placing the flowers down on a console inside her apartment.

She reaches for me, grasps the lapels of my blazer, and gives a friendly tug. I move closer to her, my hands finding her hips, my eyes pinned to hers.

"I've been thinking," she says.

"About what?"

"If we're going to give this a real go..."

My stomach tightens painfully as I wait for her next words. Does she have faith in us? Does she think we can make each other happy?

"Then we need to let go of the past. We need to move forward. Start with as much of a clean slate as possible." She releases a shaky exhale. "So, hi, I'm Harper. Harper Henderson."

My hands squeeze her hips and I grin. "I like the alliteration."

She laughs and draws me even closer. Her eyes hold mine, playful and sparkling. She bites her bottom lip and I nearly groan at the visual.

"God, I missed you, babe," I tell her the truth.

She giggles. "It's our first date, Damien."

"You've had every one of my firsts that really matters, Harp," I give her the truth.

She pulls back slightly, studies my expression. Then she shifts forward and her mouth lands on mine. She kisses me softly, testing it out carefully. It's nothing like the first night she kissed me but it's sweet. Lined with meaning, rounded out with hope.

Harper shuffles closer into my frame and I wrap my arms around her lower back, slanting my head to deepen the kiss. To show her how much I want her. Need her. Love her.

Her fingers lace behind my neck and I draw her up into my arms until I'm carrying her. I hold her close and kiss her hard, giving her my apology and desire. "I love you, Harper. I think I have from that first night on the balcony."

She smiles up at me as she slides down my body. Even once her feet are planted on the floor, I keep my arms around her. "I love you, too." Her eyes dazzle, hopping from one of my eyes to the other and back again. "Are you going to tell me your name?"

Tossing my head back, I laugh. I scoop my beautiful woman up in my arms and carry her over to her couch. "Damien Barnes."

"What do you do, Damien?"

I set her down so she can put on her heels.

"I'm a hockey player."

Her mouth drops open in mock surprise. "Really? Oh wow. I had no idea."

I snort. "You're such a goof."

She grins. "You like it."

I kiss her again, taking her shoe and slipping it onto her foot. "I fucking love it."

When her heels are strapped in place, she stands, and I take her hand.

I escort her to my car, helping her slip into the low seat. "You ready for this?" I ask as she stares up at me.

Harper's hands glide over the soft material of her dress. She arches an eyebrow. "For dinner?"

I smirk. "To be relationship goals."

She laughs. "I like your confidence, Barnes."

"I like your everything, Henderson."

She laughs as I shut the car door and slip into the driver's side. I start the car and Harper turns to me, her eyes serious. "We already are, you know?"

I turn to her and pause. "Are what?"

"Relationship goals." She reaches for my hand and laces our fingers together. "Not every guy would admit he was wrong, would take responsibility for his actions and want to try again."

"Not every woman would give the guy another shot."

"She would if she truly loved him," Harper admits quietly.

"And he would earn her trust, over and over and over again, if he was crazy in love with her." I squeeze her hand, lean across the center console to give her a quick peck. "You're the greatest treasure of my life, Harp. I won't lose you again."

She smiles and lifts her chin. "See? Relationship goals."

I chuckle and pull out of the parking garage.

Harper and I drive to dinner, toward our future, hand in hand.

And I silently vow to never let her go.

EPILOGUE

FOUR MONTHS LATER

Thanksgiving
Harper

THE SNOW FALLING OUTSIDE IS soft and peaceful. I snuggle deeper under the plaid blanket and lean my forehead against the cool pane of glass. Tucked into this window seat, I feel like I'm locked inside a snow globe, watching the magic of winter dance around me.

"You warm enough?" Charlie asks, passing me a mug of hot chocolate.

"Hey, yeah." I grin up at him and take the mug. "Thanks."

He repositions a nearby chair to face me and sits down. "Okay, so the game tonight is charades." Charlie leans forward, his elbows dropping to his knees as he gives me a serious look.

I sit up straighter in my seat.

"Damien and Garrett will be on a team. They always are. And they always ch—"

"Uncle Charlie!" Garrett yells, zooming by with his

arms outstretched, like an airplane. "Stop lying to Harper!" He stops in front of me and gives me the most adorable look. "I don't cheat!"

"I believe you," I tell him seriously.

"Uncle Damien does!" he yells, resuming his running and airplane noises.

"Hey!" Damien calls out from the nearby kitchen island. He's having a drink with his dad as Mrs. Barnes cuts the brownies she and Garrett made after dinner.

"See." Charlie nods, gesturing toward Damien and slapping his hand against his thigh. "From the mouth of a babe."

I laugh and shake my head.

"Let Harper enjoy the snow without listening to your whining," Fiona instructs Charlie.

He turns toward his sister. "Whining? I'm sorry..." He stands from his chair and moves closer to the kitchen island. "Who was complaining, just this morning, about having to drink orange juice with pulp in it?" He gives his sister a stern look.

Damien mutters something under his breath.

Mrs. Barnes pauses by the kitchen island, her eyes passing from one of her children to the next. She looks happy.

Over the past few months, my relationship with Damien's mother has changed. After Damien's and my first date, Mrs. Barnes called me to apologize. She was sincere, which I wasn't expecting. However, she admitted that between speaking with her husband, and fully acknowledging the paths her three children were barreling down, she needed to make some changes.

She decided to start with me and put in the effort to get to know me and learn about my interests. Since that first call, we started texting and chatting weekly. She began sharing recipes that Damien and I could try together. Sometimes, she forwards me articles she thinks I'll enjoy. I almost always do. When she came to see Damien play in Tennessee in September, she invited me to lunch. She was gracious and warm, and our relationship began to blossom.

As Mrs. Barnes offered insight into her world, I gained a deeper understanding of why the Barnes family is as closed off as they sometimes are. Mr. Barnes sold a chunk of his company and stepped back from a lot of the daily demands of his work. Damien's parents attend more of his games now and Mr. Barnes is even assistant coaching Garrett's soccer team.

Small changes, when taken in sum, have meant a big transition for the Barneses. There is more laughter and honesty. More joking around and confiding in each other. A lot less aloof expressions and withdrawn demeanors. They're warmer, more open with each other, and I love that I get to witness it firsthand. I love that I'm now a part of their lives.

Mrs. Barnes bites into a brownie and moans. "Garrett, we did it! These are delicious."

"Ooh, can I have one, Nana?" Garrett sits on a barstool next to Damien.

"You bet." Mrs. Barnes plates him a brownie.

Before he can take a bite, Damien snatches it and tosses the whole thing into his mouth. He chews loudly, making all sorts of humming noises about how delicious and fudgey it is.

"Uncle Damien!" Garrett huffs.

Mr. Barnes laughs. Mrs. Barnes gives Damien a look while she cuts Garrett another brownie. Her eyes swing to the window and find mine. She smiles. "Come have a brownie while they're warm, Harper."

"And before Charlie and Damien eat them all," Mr. Barnes advises. He turns in his chair. "Where did Fiona go?"

Charlie moves next to his mom in the kitchen and drops his elbows to the kitchen island. Making a phone symbol with his hand, he holds it next to his ear and shakes it, indicating she's on a call.

Charlie's been home from rehab for one month and while he's still charming and sociable, he's also more careful and thoughtful. Meeting him again was another kind of do-over, but considering he teases me like a brother, I think we're doing a good job.

Fiona waltzes into the kitchen, her skin flushed.

"What's wrong, Fi?" Mrs. Barnes asks.

Fiona grins. "I"—she shakes her head—"I have a date."

"A date?" Damien looks up.

"With whom?" Charlie demands.

"Can I have another brownie?" Garrett asks.

Mrs. Barnes rolls her eyes.

Fiona ignores their questions and looks at me. "Harper, please tell me you have something to wear that I can borrow?"

Mrs. Barnes points toward her closet. "I have a whole closet filled with dresses, Fi. Take anything you'd like."

Damien snorts. Charlie hides his laughter in his hot chocolate. Even Mr. Barnes looks amused.

"What?" Mrs. Barnes asks.

"It's a *first* date, Mom. We're grabbing drinks, not attending a ball. It certainly doesn't require some lavish number that Bethany pulled."

Mrs. Barnes laughs, taking the razzing in stride. She holds up a hand. "Okay. Okay. Tell us about this guy."

"He's...a good man. Sincere and funny. Smart," Fiona explains, gesturing with her hands.

"He lives here, in Aspen?"

She nods.

"How did you meet?" Mr. Barnes inquires.

Fiona blushes. "Online."

"What did we tell you about going into those chat rooms?" Charlie mock scolds, a hand on his hip.

"What does he do?" Mrs. Barnes asks, more curious than concerned.

Fiona looks at me and I slip from the window seat.

"I have several options. We'll pull together something cute." I pick up my hot chocolate.

"Fiona," Damien sings. "Tell us what he does for a living. Is he from 'good stock'?" He air quotes.

Mrs. Barnes whips a dish towel at him.

"We need his family name," Charlie agrees, pulling out his phone.

"And his taxes from the last three years," Damien tacks on.

"How tall is he? Can you wear heels?" Charlie inquires.

"All right, enough, enough." Mrs. Barnes laughs. "I was awful, okay? I know it and I'm sorry."

All the Barnes men and Fiona pause and stare at Mrs. Barnes.

She points her fork at them and admits, "That's the only time I'm going to say it too."

A silence hovers over the table before everyone cracks up, teasing Mrs. Barnes. She laughs with them, her cheeks rosy, her eyes dancing. She looks like a completely different version of the woman I met over the summer and since I saw her transformation happen over the past four months, it's lovely to know she's in a much better place.

I laugh and tip my head toward Damien's and my bedroom.

Damien catches my eye as I pass him, blowing me a kiss, his eyes filled with gratitude.

I blow him a kiss back.

Garrett fake gags.

"Now we have to redo our teams for charades," Charlie mumbles, like his entire evening is falling apart.

Fiona and I disappear into my bedroom and spend the next forty minutes putting together outfits and laughing as she fills me in on her date with a handsome, considerate, down-to-earth ski instructor and part-time mechanic she's been speaking to for weeks. She looks happy and as I push my favorite pair of jeans into her hands, I'm happy for her.

After Fiona leaves, the family settles around the fire for an intense game of charades. There are snacks and hot chocolate. Laughter and teasing. It's the kind of family game night I used to have as a kid, with my brother and me ganging up on our parents and trying to stay up past our bedtimes.

It fills me with nostalgia but also hope that one day, Damien and I will grow a family and it will be like this. Cozy nights wrapped in blankets, with hot chocolates in hand and sore bellies from endless laughter.

After Damien and Garrett secure their win, Damien whisks me to our bedroom. We ignore Charlie's obnoxious whistles as the door closes behind us.

Damien turns off the lights, the moonlight streaming in through the big windows, reflecting off the snow outside. It casts everything in a warm glow.

Damien crosses his arms and leans back against the door as I quietly undress. When I'm clad in a black bra and panties, he rushes me, scooping me into his arms and laying me out on the bed.

Breathless laughter bubbles up inside as Damien lands on top of me. Automatically, my legs wrap around his hips, and he settles into the space above me. He pulls off his shirt and brushes my hair from my face. When he stares down at me, his gaze is reverent.

"Thank you for tonight, with my family," he says softly.

"Thank you for bringing me skiing in Aspen," I quip back.

He snorts, rubs the end of his nose against mine. "I love you, Harper Henderson."

I bite my bottom lip. "Show me how much."

"Always," he agrees, drawing me into a kiss.

Then he sets to work and shows me the depths of his feelings, the intensity of his desire, the sincerity of his love.

He shows me again and again and again.

I lose myself in his touch. I free-fall into the bottomless pools of his gaze. I let his kiss consume me.

When we're spent and sated, we fall asleep, our bodies pressed tightly together, surrounded by a wonderland of our own making.

It's a hell of a lot more than relationship goals.

Together, Damien Barnes and I are everything.

———

THANK you so much for reading *Playboy's Reward*! I hope you fell in love with Damien and Harper's journey. If second chance romances (and military romance vibes!) are your jam, pre-order Beau and Celine's book, *Hero's Risk*, coming January 5.

ACKNOWLEDGMENTS

Thank you so much to all who contributed to Damien and Harper's journey — from the first outline to release day!

Melissa Panio-Peterson, Sheila Dohmann, Amy Parsons, Erica Russikoff, Becca Mysoor, Dani Sanchez and the Wildfire Team, Virginia Carey, and Amber — all of my thanks and gratitude for your constant support and love!

For the covers of this series, I had the wonderful opportunity to work with Niagara-based photographer Stephanie Iannacchino (www.stecchinoo.com) and these fantastic athletes, and now, cover models: Justin, Manny, Evan, Brady, and Tony.

While I'm grateful to all for their collaboration, I'm particularly thankful for my husband Tony for showing up, doing two-a-days, and committing to be my cover model for *Playboy's Reward.* Damien's character is inspired by him and it was so fun to do a photoshoot together!

To the readers and bloggers, the early reviewers and bookstagrammers, the entire BookTok community — THANK YOU! Thank you for picking up my book babies and falling in love with these characters and the family they form. Your support means everything to me.

To Tony and our babies — wouldn't want to take this ride with anyone else. Y'all are my world.

ALSO BY GINA AZZI

Healing My Heart

The Kane Brothers Series:

Rescuing Broken (Jax's Story)

Recovering Beauty (Carter's Story)

Reclaiming Brave (Denver's Story)

My Christmas Wish

(A Kane Family Christmas

+ *One Last Chance* FREE prequel)

Finding Love in Scotland Series:

My Christmas Wish

(A Kane Family Christmas

+ *One Last Chance* FREE prequel)

One Last Chance (Daisy and Finn)

This Time Around (Aaron and Everly)

One Great Love

The College Pact Series:

The Last First Game (Lila's Story)

Kiss Me Goodnight in Rome (Mia's Story)

All the While (Maura's Story)

Me + You (Emma's Story)

Standalone

Corner of Ocean and Bay

Made in the USA
Monee, IL
23 July 2023